Human Interest Stories

from

Antietam

Scott L. Mingus, Sr.

COLECRAFT INDUSTRIES

Since 1981

Published by Colecraft Industries
970 Mt. Carmel Road
Orrtanna, PA 17353

The author wishes to thank the staff of the U.S. Army Military History Institute, who provided leads on materials in their library and files, as did the staff of the Antietam National Battlefield, including park ranger Alann Schmidt. Gerard Mayers proofread the manuscript and offered several useful suggestions. Most of all, thanks to my beloved wife, Debi Mingus, for her support and encouragement!

ISBN 0-9777125-32

For more information visit our website: www.colecraftbooks.com

To contact us via e-mail send to: colecraftbooks@aol.com

First Edition

PRINTED AND BOUND IN THE UNITED STATES OF AMERICA

Cover design by Philip M. Cole

Contents

Introduction   4

Chronology: Timeline of the Maryland Campaign   5

Chapter One: The Confederates Invade Maryland   6

Chapter Two: South Mountain and Harper's Ferry   29

Chapter Three: Antietam   44

Chapter Four: The Aftermath   78

Sorrow and pain and hatred will go,
Sharpness of death – that, too, will cease,
Out of the agony, roses grow;
Out of the heart-ache, in finite peace.

- Irene Fowler Brown

Introduction

While the Battle of Gettysburg and the concurrent Vicksburg Campaign often are designated as the "High Water Mark of the Confederacy," in some ways, it can be argued that its true high water mark was the late summer of 1862. Confederate fortunes were on the rise across the entire country, and Union hopes for an early end to the war had long since faded. In the western theater, Rebel forces were advancing across a wide front. In the East, reinforced by fresh brigades, Gen. Robert E. Lee was coming off one of his most spectacular victories, having smashed the Federal army of Maj. Gen. John Pope at Second Manassas. Lee's soldiers were by now convinced that the man they had once disparaged as "Granny Lee" for his earlier cautiousness was actually a military genius, and that his Army of Northern Virginia was invincible.

Lee and one of his chief subordinates, Thomas J. "Stonewall" Jackson, had for some time contemplated invading the North. During the Valley Campaign in May 1862, Jackson had informed a Confederate congressman that, if he had 40,000 men, he would "raise the siege of Richmond and transfer this campaign to the banks of the Susquehanna," a broad river flowing through central Pennsylvania. The hoped for reinforcements were not forthcoming, and Jackson's command was later ordered to Virginia to assist Lee during the Peninsula Campaign. With his late August triumph at Second Manassas, Lee believed that the opportunity had now arrived. He soon headed northward to draw the war away from Virginia and to bolster his ranks with expected Maryland recruits.

The ensuing Maryland Campaign resulted in a series of marches and engagements, leading to the bloodiest single day in American military history – the Battle of Antietam (or Sharpsburg to many Southerners), with over 23,000 casualties. Dozens of books have more than adequately covered the military aspects of the campaign, but only a handful have tackled the human equation. This work, a companion to the earlier *Human Interest Stories of the Gettysburg Campaign*, illustrates the campaign through a series of anecdotes and incidents that exemplify the humor, pathos, irony, and human interest stories of the Maryland Campaign. The reader will find some material that may be familiar, but will also discover several obscure incidents that have been out of print since the nineteenth century.

These accounts have been compiled mainly from old regimental histories, mostly published in the four decades following the war. Others are taken from letters, diaries, period newspapers, and other primary sources. All are presumed to be true, although it must be admitted that the veterans' memories and recollections tended to fade (or be exaggerated) with the passage of time. In any event, they are reflective of the spirit of the common soldier of the Civil War – men who left their homes, families, sweethearts, and livelihoods to serve in the opposing armies; some to pursue a dream, some to fulfill political or social ambitions, and some for adventure or personal glory.

It is to these men whose "hearts were touched with fire," as well as the civilians of Maryland whose homes and businesses were affected by warfare, that this book is dedicated. It is also dedicated to the memory of the Chambers brothers of the Seventh (West) Virginia, my great-great uncles, who survived the horror of the attack on Antietam's "Bloody Lane," and to my beloved father, Staff Sgt. Robert E. Mingus, a decorated veteran of WWII.

Chronology of the 1862 Maryland Campaign

September 2 – Fresh off its stunning victory at Second Manassas, Robert E. Lee's Army of Northern Virginia concentrates near Chantilly, Virginia. George B. McClellan is restored to command of the Federal Army of the Potomac.

September 3 – Lee notifies Jefferson Davis that he will cross the Potomac River into Maryland unless the president objects. None forthcoming, Lee begins shifting his army north and west from Chantilly towards Leesburg, Virginia.

September 4 – Lee's cavalry under J.E.B. Stuart splashes across the Potomac River into Maryland, followed by the infantry division of D. H. Hill.

September 5 – McClellan begins to move his Union army northward from Washington D.C. in pursuit of Lee. Still more Confederates cross the Potomac.

September 7 – The main body of the Confederate army reaches Frederick, Maryland. The next day, Lee issues a proclamation calling on Marylanders to support the Confederacy.

September 12 – Stonewall Jackson's Confederates begin to invest Harper's Ferry.

September 13 – Most of the Union army arrives in Frederick, and then moves towards South Mountain after McClellan is given a lost Confederate dispatch outlining various enemy movements and locations.

September 14 – Federals attack Confederates defending three strategic gaps on South Mountain, but fail to quickly penetrate into the valley beyond. D. H. Hill's determined defense buys Jackson enough time to surround Harper's Ferry.

September 15 – Jackson skillfully places his artillery on the heights surrounding Harper's Ferry, bombards the town, and forces the surrender of over 12,000 Union defenders.

September 16 – The opposing armies concentrate at Sharpsburg, and a sharp skirmish occurs in the East Woods in the evening. McClellan repositions for a morning attack.

September 17 – The Battle of Antietam results in over 23,000 casualties, the "bloodiest day" in American military history.

September 19 – Lee's rear guard is attacked at Shepherdstown, Virginia; a heavy counterattack by A. P. Hill the following day drives the Federals back across the river into Maryland. Federal pursuit is discouraged; Lee slips deeper into Virginia with his battered army. McClellan essentially stays put around Sharpsburg until well into October.

Chapter 1

The Confederates Invade Maryland

September 1 - 10, 1862

Following the 1862 Northern Virginia Campaign and its climatic Second Battle of Manassas in late August, Confederate Gen. Robert E. Lee concentrated his Army of Northern Virginia around the hamlet of Chantilly, Virginia, in early September. Fresh reinforcements had essentially offset his recent losses, and Lee believed that the timing was right for an invasion of the North. He wanted to spare the local farmers from the burden of feeding the opposing armies. In addition, belief was strong at the highest levels of the Confederate War Department that as many as 25-30,000 Marylanders might join Lee's army as it passed through the border state. A few officials even thought that Maryland might join the Confederacy. Lee began to bring together the scattered elements of his army in preparation for the planned invasion.

On September 1, Brig. Gen. John Bell Hood and his division, including the famed Texas Brigade, received orders to march with Lt. Gen. James Longstreet's command northeast along the Warrenton Turnpike toward Centreville, Virginia. Hood's column included several new, fully equipped Union ambulances that had been captured by his men at the close of the Second Battle of Manassas, just two days before. Believing he had formal command of Hood's force as well as his own brigade, Maj. Gen. Nathan "Shank" or "Shanks" Evans ordered Hood to turn over these prized ambulances to his own North Carolina troops. Hood did not recognize Evans' current authority over his division and refused the direct order. Evans immediately placed the junior officer under arrest and reported the incident to General Longstreet, who ordered Hood to travel to the rear to Culpeper Courthouse, Virginia, to await trial.

General Lee soon countermanded Longstreet's order, as he needed all his generals for the move northward into Maryland, but Hood remained under arrest and marched at the rear of his column in disgrace. Days later, not far from South Mountain, Hood heard the Texas Brigade in his front repeatedly chant "Give us Hood!" When he approached Lee, the latter told Hood that he did not wish to enter battle "with one of [his] best officers under arrest." He offered to revoke the charges if Hood would express regret over the ambulance incident. Hood refused to do so, but Lee suspended the inquiry for the duration of the impending campaign. The issue was never again raised by Lee, and Hood was given back his side arms and horse.

G. Moxley Sorrel, *At the Right Hand of Longstreet: Recollections of a Confederate Staff Officer*. (New York and Washington: The Neale Publishing Company, 1905).

**

On September 3, Lee's army headed north towards Leesburg, Virginia, and nearby fords across the Potomac River leading to Maryland. On September 4, the first elements of Maj. Gen. J.E.B. Stuart's cavalry splashed across White's Ford, followed soon by Maj. Gen. D. H. Hill's infantry division. By September 7, most of Lee's army had entered the "Old Line State." Regiments were often serenaded with the strains of *Maryland, My Maryland* as they waded across the broad, chilly river, but, to the surprise of many Confederate officers, few Marylanders actually took up arms and joined the Southern forces. Lee, whose hands and wrists had been badly injured in a fall, could not ride his horse and, instead, crossed the river in an ambulance, an inglorious way for the Confederacy's most celebrated leader to enter Northern soil.

The War of the Rebellion: A Compilation of the Official Records of the Union and Confederate Armies, 70 volumes in 4 series. Washington, D.C.: United States Government Printing Office, 1880-1901.

G. Moxley Sorrel, *At the Right Hand of Longstreet: Recollections of a Confederate Staff Officer.* (New York and Washington: The Neale Publishing Company, 1905).

**

Not all of Lee's soldiers were anxious to enter Maryland. Some who had enlisted strictly to defend the Confederacy against Federal aggression were not willing to invade the North. Others were too exhausted or ill from the grueling Northern Virginia Campaign. General Lee had issued orders that all sick and shoeless men should remain in Virginia when the army marched northward, assembling at Leesburg and then accompanying the wagon trains to Winchester. In Pvt. David Johnston's opinion, this was an "idiotic proclamation," as it gave credence to any slacker who wanted to remain behind. Rapid marching, eleven pitched battles in just ninety days, insufficient food and clothing, and illness had created a small army of stragglers (by some estimates over 10,000 men). Johnston reported a great many that were not sick or barefoot had remained at Leesburg because of their aversion to fighting beyond Virginia, north of the Potomac. Many in his own regiment, the Seventh Virginia, were among these less stalwart souls who chose the comforts of the Old Dominion versus the hazards of another campaign. Several actually threw away their shoes to avoid the upcoming invasion. Johnston, despite being barefoot himself, was among the thousands of Lee's warriors that managed to keep up with the army as it marched into Maryland and destiny.

David E. Johnston, *The Story of a Confederate Boy in the Civil War.* (Portland, Oregon: Glass & Prudhomme Company, 1914).

**

Newspapers were a precious commodity to most Civil War soldiers. Papers from home often helped them feel a connection with the daily affairs of friends and families on the home front. Enemy newspapers at times could be gleaned for tidbits on troop movements, morale, and similar items of interest to military strategists. Once the paper had been passed around the regiment or battery, it was normally consigned to other utilitarian uses. For one foot soldier in the Seventeenth Virginia in Kemper's Brigade, a copy of the New York *World* proved to be invaluable as he wearily tramped towards Maryland. Discovering that his oilcloth had been stolen, he had begged the newspaper from a comrade and used it for two weeks as a makeshift ground cover when he slept, keeping him reasonably dry from the evening dews and damps. Every morning, he would rise and carefully refold the paper, like "a lawyer his parchment, or a beauty her curl papers." However, he was much dismayed when a hard rain one night turned the newspaper into a mush of soggy pulp. With incipient tears in his eyes, he turned to his comrades and intoned that he "would always cherish a tender feeling for the New York *World* so long as the bullets might spare him."

Alexander Hunter, *Johnny Reb and Billy Yank.* (New York and Washington: The Neale Publishing Company, 1905).

**

Lee's manpower had been reduced during the Northern Virginia Campaign, but the losses had since been replenished and confidence abounded. What did not abound were rations for his men. They subsisted primarily on roasted corn and green apples, as provisions were scarce in the pine thickets and barren red clay gullies of Prince William County. As the Confederate army headed northward into Loudoun County towards Leesburg and beyond to Maryland, their heavily laden supply wagons were slow to keep up. Huge quantities of captured Federal supplies had been burned at Manassas Junction, and many hungry men longed for the carloads of delicacies they had torched.

By the time Maj. Gen. Lafayette McLaws' veteran division went into bivouac near Leesburg, hunger had got the better of the men's morals, and many of them (against Lee's strict orders) raided a nearby large cornfield for rations. The concerned farmer soon called on McLaws to protect his private property. The obliging general ordered sentries to surround the field, arrest every man coming out with corn, and bring him and his plunder to headquarters. It was not long until the crestfallen thieves began to appear, under armed guard, before the irate commander. As each one, with his armload of corn, halted before him, McLaws roared, "Where did you get that corn?" The nervous culprit would usually begin, "Why, General, I had nothing to eat for three days, and I didn't know when the wagons would come," but there the angry general stopped him with the sharp order: "Put it down there on the ground and go join your command immediately!"

As other thieves periodically arrived and heard McLaws' stern query, each man seemingly always uttered the same excuses – "hungry," "wagons have not come up yet," etc. In each case, McLaws' stern order was "throw it down on that pile and go join your command." This oft-repeated process soon caused quite a large mound of confiscated corn to grow in front of McLaws' quarters. Finally, one Rebel in the Fifty-second Virginia, who had caught on to the manner and form of the proceedings, was escorted to McLaws and accosted with the usual, "What are you going to do with that corn?" Expecting the same tired explanation, McLaws was surprised when the man began to imitate him. "Why, sir," briskly responded the clever culprit, "I'm going to throw it down on that pile thar, and go and join my command, immejitly, I am!" The general broke down, the guards roared, and the witty Reb quietly slipped away "immejitly." An amused

McLaws ordered his brigade quartermaster to take charge of the corn and issue it to his men, who made it last until the wagons finally arrived with rations.

John S. Robson, *How a One-Legged Rebel Lives: Reminiscences of the Civil War.* (Durham, North Carolina: The Educator Co., 1898).

**

To one malnourished Virginian, the steady diet was becoming monotonous: "Our menu consisted of apples and corn. We toasted, we burned, we stewed, we boiled, we roasted these two together, and singly, until there was not a man whose form had not caved in, and who had not a bad attack of diarrhea." Discarded newspapers again found more utilitarian purposes.

Alexander Hunter, "A High Private's Account of the Battle of Sharpsburg," *Southern Historical Society Papers*, Vol. X (Richmond, Virginia: 1882).

**

The day before Stonewall Jackson's wing of the army forded the Potomac River, the Fifty-fifth Virginia marched through Leesburg. Lt. Robert Healy and his company encountered an old lady, who, with tears in her eyes and uplifted hands, emotionally exclaimed: "The Lord bless your dirty ragged souls!" Healy added, "[I] don't think we were any dirtier than the rest, but it was our luck to get the blessing."

Henry K. Douglas, "Stonewall Jackson in Maryland," *Battles and Leaders of the Civil War*, Volume II. (New York: The Century Co., 1887-88).

**

After wading the Potomac at White's Ford and entering Maryland on September 5, the Twenty-first Virginia marched a short distance up the towpath of the Chesapeake & Ohio Canal to the locks. There, the men and wagons crossed the deep canal on a bridge before marching northward the rest of the day to the village of Three Springs. After another hard march the next day, the veteran regiment tramped by the Baltimore & Ohio Railroad depot near Frederick, where they discovered several wooden boxcars loaded with fresh watermelons. Several soldiers broke ranks and raided the railcars before scurrying back to their places in the ranks. As the long gray column entered the city, many men carefully cradled melons in their arms. They marched to the fairgrounds, which had previously been retrofitted by the Federal army as a large hospital and campsite. The exhausted Virginians stacked arms and made themselves comfortable for the evening. Eagerly, they shared slices of the ripe juicy fruit, a delicacy many had not eaten since entering the service. It was a refreshing change from their diet of roasted Indian corn, green apples, and unsalted boiled beef.

John H. Worsham, *One of Jackson's Foot Cavalry: His Experience and What He Saw During the War 1861-1865*...(New York: The Neale Publishing Company, 1912).

**

As the Troup Artillery forded the Potomac River on September 6, the Georgians were accompanied by their beloved mascot, "Charlie." While the battery was stationed at Staunton, Virginia, on the afternoon of August 1, 1861, a "small and uncouth" dog had wandered into their camp. Possessed of a genial disposition, the amiable mutt had endeared himself to the artillerymen. He was invited to spend the night and was given a bountiful supper and a comfortable bed by the campfire. The following morning, as the battery took up the line of march, the little pooch "signified his desire to become an independent member of the company, and was cordially accepted..." He had stayed with the artillerymen for over a year, through the marching and fighting of the Peninsula and Northern Virginia campaigns. Pvt. George Atkisson later wrote, "He seemed to enjoy the whistling of bullets, shrieking of shells, and to go wild with delight as the combat raged. He was too small to take an active part in the work, but would dart back and forth from gun to gun, cheering the men with his clear, ringing voice, which could be heard distinctly above the din of the battle. In the body of this little four-legged comrade beat a warm, affectionate heart."

Now, as the Georgians splashed across the Potomac, Charlie was placed atop the foremost caisson for safety, the river being too wide and swift for him to swim. As the team of horses reached the Maryland shore, Charlie happily sprang to the ground, the first one of the company to set foot on Northern soil. There on the riverbank, he danced and barked with delight until the last gun had safely crossed. He then trotted alongside the crewmen as they marched through Maryland.

George B. Atkisson, "Charlie: 'Recruit' to Troup Artillery." (*Confederate Veteran,* Vol. XIX).

**

As Brig. Gen. James Kemper's veteran brigade waded across the Potomac into Maryland, most of the members of the Seventeenth Virginia stripped off their clothes. They carried them and their muskets above their heads as they carefully sloshed across the worn river bottom. Some were denuded only from the waist down; a few others crossed without taking off their garments and were now lying in the sun on the Maryland side trying to dry out their clothes. Half-naked warriors daintily sought to protect their tattered rags while they tried to avoid slipping on the rocks – the unusual scene was comical to at least one participant. Pvt. Alexander Hunter wrote, "It was a genial, joyous, side-splitting evolution, that crossing over. The gravest man in America sitting on that shore watching the proceedings would have laughed until tears rolled down his saturnine face... the very fishes opened their broad mouths, and the rooks cawed until they were hoarse, and the mules gave prolonged snorts of infinite satisfaction."

Alexander Hunter, *Johnny Reb and Billy Yank*. (New York and Washington: The Neale Publishing Company, 1905).

**

While the Confederates entered Maryland, Federal troops were beginning to respond and move in pursuit. At 7:00 a.m. on September 6, the Thirty-Sixth Ohio left Arlington, Virginia, and marched into Washington, finally halting along Pennsylvania Avenue in front of the White House and stacking their arms. A number of citizens and government officials noticed the arrival of the dusty column and came out to see them. Upon the command, "Break ranks!" the soldiers scattered in all directions to explore the nation's capital. It happened that Governor William Dennison of the Buckeye State was calling at the White House, along with Governor Francis H. Pierpont of the Union-controlled portion of Virginia (later to become the new state of West Virginia). Dennison, hearing that an Ohio regiment was outside, soon emerged from the White House with President Abraham Lincoln at his side.

Wisely, someone tipped off the regiment's colonel, George Crook, who quickly ordered his buglers to sound the assembly. As if by magic, blue-clad soldiers suddenly appeared from everywhere, their explorations of the capital cut short by the demanding bugle calls. Two swift-moving Buckeyes, one toting a large watermelon under his arm, were being closely pursued by an angry Washington policeman. The soldiers won the footrace, reaching the gun stacks and their comrades before the "cop" could lay hands on them. The patrolman soon arrived and demanded the surrender of the stolen melon. In an instant, the ripe watermelon was dropped to the ground, smashing into pieces that were quickly snatched up and gobbled down by nearby soldiers. Shepherded by Colonel Crook, they threw away the rinds, grabbed their rifles, and presented arms to the assembled dignitaries as if nothing unusual had just happened.

Old Abe had witnessed the entire episode. For some time, the president stood with his shoulders leaning on an ornamental iron fence and laughed heartily at the strange events. Perhaps not by coincidence, the quick-thinking Crook was soon promoted by Lincoln to brigadier general, with his commission dating from the day of the "great melon chase."

D. Cunningham and W. W. Miller, *Antietam: Report of the Ohio Battlefield Commission.* (Springfield, Ohio: Springfield Publishing Company, 1904).

**

A fair number of the Union regiments assembled in Washington were relatively new, comprised primarily of raw recruits that had not yet experienced battle. The Sixteenth Connecticut was one of these rookie regiments. Organized in Hartford in late August 1862 with 1,010 eager volunteers, including many of the wealthy and learned of that city, the three-year regiment was commanded by a crusty old Regular Army officer, Col. Peter Beach. Nearly all of the new soldiers "had been reared in abundance" and had "led the quiet and easy life of a citizen." Unaccustomed to hard physical labor and the soldier's outdoor lifestyle, men sweltered in their new woolen uniforms and collapsed in the August heat. Several died of sunstroke and other maladies as Beach and his officers tried transforming the gentry into fighting men.

On August 28, with the initial military drills finally over, the new troops proudly marched through Hartford's city streets in a procession led by the mayor and other dignitaries. Thousands of cheering spectators encouraged the parade of soldiers, who then embarked on two steamers for the ocean voyage to New York City. After a hearty breakfast of steaming vegetable soup and hot coffee, the joyous New Englanders marched to the rail depot in Elizabeth, New Jersey. From there, the regiment rode to Harrisburg, Pennsylvania, where they switched trains for the southward ride through the night to Baltimore. Arriving at 9 a.m., the tired, but enthusiastic soldiers were treated to "an excellent breakfast." While waiting at the depot for yet another train to take them to Washington, D.C., the welcome report was received that Stonewall Jackson had been captured. The regiment cheered and shouted, laughed and danced, rejoiced and gave thanks in the same breath. Two weeks later, they would find to their chagrin that Stonewall Jackson was very much a free man, but, for now, their joy was unbridled.

So far, for the elite of Hartford County, Connecticut, war was a lark and soldiering was fun. Things began to change quickly. They were herded into a "miserable, dirty train" for the short jaunt to the nation's capital. They arrived at Fort Ward and soon got their first glimpse of the horrors of real warfare – a long line of horse-drawn ambulances, carrying moaning men wounded at Second Bull Run, passed by the suddenly somber soldiers. That night it rained terribly. The tents not having come up, the city boys were compelled to sit in the downpour all night; to one man, it was "soldiering with a vengeance." The gloss and sheen of the infantry had been replaced with the grim reality that the picnic was now over. Within a few days, the Sixteenth Connecticut marched from Washington to catch up with the Army of the Potomac en route to Maryland. For many, their destiny was death or injury.

B. F. Blakeslee, *History of the Sixteenth Connecticut Volunteers.* (Hartford: Case, Lockwood and Brainard Co., 1875).

**

Twenty-five-year-old Sgt. George Bernard of the Twelfth Virginia (of Mahone's Brigade) had completely worn out his tattered remnants of shoes during the Northern Virginia Campaign. Shortly after Second Manassas, Capt. Nat Osborne handed the former attorney and school teacher a pair of new boots, in all probability procured from some lifeless body on that battlefield. Bernard tried them on and wore them as his regiment departed for Maryland. However, the stiff boots soon made his feet quite sore, as they were "as unyielding as if made of cast iron" as he climbed several hills.

Bernard soon decided that being barefoot would be much less painful. He tied the shoelaces together and dangled the boots from his blanket roll as he marched along the turnpike. He only wore them again when his feet were cold and when he waded across the Potomac at Edward's Ford, believing that the leather soles would protect his feet against any sharp-edged stones in the riverbed. Once on the Maryland riverbank, the boots returned to their place on the blanket roll. Days later, Bernard finally procured shoes that fit from the quartermaster and passed the rigid boots on to a comrade, who in turn passed them on to another man, and he to yet another soldier. Sergeant Bernard would be wounded and captured in the fighting at South Mountain on September 14, taking his new shoes and crutches with him into captivity at Baltimore and later at Fort Monroe in Virginia.

George S. Bernard, *Addresses delivered before A.P. Hill Camp of Confederate Veterans, of Petersburg, Va.* (Petersburg, Virginia: Fenn & Owen, 1892).

**

Crossing the broad Potomac was at times comical. A short, slight Irishman in Company C of the Eighteenth Mississippi, Tommy Brennan, prepared to cross the half-mile-wide river at Shepherdstown's Packhorse Ford. He held his musket, cartridge box, and shoes above his head as he waded across the chilly river. He was only twenty yards from Maryland when he smugly called back to his comrades, "Boys, I am over dry shod!" Brennan had no sooner looked back when he suddenly disappeared from view. He had stepped into a deep hole in the riverbed and tumbled under, head and ears, gun and all.

Captain James Dinkins, *1861-1865 by an Old Johnnie: Personal Recollections and Experiences in the Confederate Army.* (Cincinnati: The Robert Clarke Company, 1897).

**

The residents of Maryland, a border state, had decidedly different loyalties towards the opposing armies and their underlying politics. A large portion of the population was ambivalent towards both sides, simply wanting to be left alone to their business. Many citizens hid everything of value so that neither military force could steal it. Capt. Greenlee Davidson, commander of Letcher's Battery of Virginia artillery, wrote home, "The lands are in the highest state of cultivation and every farm has a barn almost as large as Noah's Ark. But strange to say, none of these magnificent barns, or roomy smokehouses, contain neither corn nor meat…" Most of the tidy farmhouses were deserted, but when the artillerymen encountered the remaining residents, they were told that they had nothing to sell. Davison concluded, "It is perfectly evident that the people of this section of the State are as hostile to us as if we were north of [the] Mason and Dixon line."

Charles W. Turner, editor, *Captain Greenlee Davidson, C.S.A.: Diary and Letters 1851-1863.* (Verona, Virginia: McClure Press, 1975).

**

Such was not the case in Poolesville, where several young Marylanders enlisted on the spot and joined the Confederate cavalry, among them two shopkeepers who freely opened their establishments to two passing brigades. Business was brisk, especially shoes and boots, which flew off the shelves, as well as cigars, lemons, and pocketknives, all favorites with the Rebel officers. Now enriched with considerable

Confederate script, the two businessmen saddled their horses and followed Fitz Lee and Wade Hampton's troopers out of town, determined to get in on the coming action.

Heros von Borcke, *Memoirs of the Confederate War for Independence*. (New York: Peter Smith, 1938).

**

In one central Maryland town, a group of gushing ladies encircled Stonewall Jackson as he rode by and began cutting off the buttons from his coat. He genially remarked, "Ladies, this is the first time I was ever surrounded." However, when they began snipping fabric from his pants, "it was feared he would be in the uniform of a Georgia Colonel, minus all except a shirt collar and spurs. For once he was badly scared."

Richmond *Daily Dispatch*, September 29, 1862.

**

As the Seventeenth Virginia marched through Frederick on September 6, one citizen took pity on a barefooted Rebel infantryman who painfully limped by. He stopped the struggling soldier, took off his own shoes, and pressed them into the startled Confederate's hands.

Alexander Hunter, *Johnny Reb and Billy Yank*. (New York and Washington: The Neale Publishing Company, 1905).

**

As the lengthy Confederate parade passed through Frederick, many soldiers were able to pause long enough to call upon the town's merchants. One incredulous tobacconist was particularly pleased, as he sold out his entire inventory for $30,000 within a day. As he had paid only $10,000 for the stock, he was greedily counting his windfall profit. However, most of his receipts were in Confederate money, which would prove to be valueless not long afterwards. Other merchants also fared well, selling large quantities of lager beer, ice cream, dates, preserves, and confectioneries. Soldiers raced to purchase items selling at pre-war peacetime prices, a rarity in Virginia, but commonplace in Frederick, where gouging did not begin until a couple of days later when demand finally outstripped supply. Coffee at a quarter a pound was a best seller, as were shoes at $3 a pair and salt at fifty cents a sack.

Richmond *Daily Dispatch*, September 22, 1862.
John Esten Cooke, *The Life of Stonewall Jackson*. (New York: Charles B. Richardson, 1863).

**

The young women of Maryland made an impression on several Confederates as Lee's army marched northward. Pvt. James Johnston of the Eleventh Mississippi wrote to his fiancée that, "The ladies around Frederick are quite pretty, but towards Hagerstown, being almost entirely Dutch, they were tidy but exceedingly homely."

James S. Johnston, September 22, 1862, letter to Mary Green (Mercer Green Johnston Collection, Manuscripts Division, Library of Congress).

**

In turn, the Confederates must have made quite an impression themselves on the ladies of Maryland. Tired, dirty, unkempt, malodorous in many cases, and often barefooted, the soldiers trudged along toward an unseen destiny north of the Mason-Dixon Line. Few presented any semblance of military uniformity or precision, yet by the fall of 1862, Lee's army had become one of the world's finest fighting forces, despite the men's outward appearance.

According to Pvt. David Johnston of the Seventh Virginia, "A musket, cartridge box with forty rounds of cartridges, cloth haversack, blanket and canteen made up the Confederate soldier's equipment. No man was allowed a change of clothing, nor could he have carried it. A gray cap, jacket, trousers and colored shirt – calico mostly – made up a private's wardrobe. When a clean shirt became necessary, we took off the soiled one, went to the water, usually without soap, gave it a little rubbing, and if the sun was shining, hung the shirt on a bush to dry, while the wearer sought the shade to give the shirt a chance. The method of carrying our few assets was to roll them in a blanket, tying each end of the roll, which was then swung over the shoulder. At night this blanket was unrolled and wrapped around its owner, who found a place on the ground with his cartridge box for a pillow. We cooked but little, having usually little to cook. The frying pan was in use, if we had one."

David E. Johnston, *The Story of a Confederate Boy in the Civil War.* (Portland, Oregon: Glass & Prudhomme Company, 1914).

**

One Frederick lady wrote a friend with her own impressions of the unwelcome guests from Dixie. "Their coming was unheralded by any pomp and pageant whatever. No bursts of martial music greeted your ear, no thundering sound of cannon, no brilliant staff, no glittering cortege dashed through the streets; instead came three long dirty columns that kept on in an unceasing flow. I could scarcely believe my eyes; was this body of men moving so smoothly along, with no order, their guns carried in every fashion, no two dressed alike, their officers hardly distinguishable from the privates – were these, I asked myself in amazement, were these dirty, lank, ugly specimens of humanity, with shocks of hair sticking through the holes in their hats, and the dust thick on their dirty faces, the men that had coped and encountered successfully, and driven back again and again our splendid legions with their fine discipline, their martial show and colour, their solid battalions keeping such perfect time to the inspiring bands of music?

I must confess, Minnie, that I felt humiliated at the thought that this horde of ragamuffins could set our grand army of the Union at defiance. Why it seems as if a single regiment of our gallant boys in blue could drive that dirty crew in the river without any trouble. And then, too, I wish you could see how they behaved – a crowd of boys on a holiday don't seem happier. They are on the broad grin all the time. Oh! They are so dirty! I don't think the Potomac River could wash them clean; and ragged! – There is not a scarecrow in the cornfields that would not scorn to exchange clothes with them; and so tattered!

There isn't a decently dressed soldier in their whole army. I saw some strikingly handsome faces though; or, rather, they would have been so if they could have had a good scrubbing. They were very polite, I must confess, and always asked for a drink of water, or anything else, and never think of coming inside of a door without an invitation. Many of them were bare footed. Indeed I felt sorry for the poor, misguided wretches, for some were limping along so painfully, trying hard to keep with their comrades."

Alexander Hunter, "The Battle of Antietam or Sharpsburg," *Southern Historical Society Papers*, Vol. X. (Richmond, Virginia: 1882).

**

Lee's army maintained amazing discipline while sojourning in Frederick According to one of J.E.B. Stuart's staff officers, John Esten Cooke, "Though thousands of soldiers are now roaming through the town, there has not been a solitary instance of misdemeanor. I have heard no shouting, no clamor of any kind, and seen but a single case of intoxication – a one-legged Yankee prisoner."

John Esten Cooke, *The Life of Stonewall Jackson*. (New York: Charles B. Richardson, 1863).

**

Lee's army lingered a few days around Frederick to rest, recruit, and procure provisions. On Sunday evening (September 7), Stonewall Jackson went into Frederick City for the first time, expressing a keen desire to attend church. As there was no service at the local Presbyterian Church, he instead went to the German Reformed Church, which was open for evening worship. According to staff officer Lt. Henry K. Douglas, "As usual, [Jackson] fell asleep, but this time more soundly than was his wont. His head sunk upon his breast, his cap dropped from his hands to the floor, the prayers of the congregation did not disturb him, and only the choir and the deep-toned organ awakened him. Afterward I learned that the minister was credited with much loyalty and courage because he had prayed for the President of the United States in the very presence of Stonewall Jackson. Well, the general didn't hear the prayer, and, if he had, he would doubtless have felt like replying as General Ewell did, when asked at Carlisle, Pennsylvania, if he would permit the usual prayer for President Lincoln – 'Certainly; I'm sure he needs it.'"

Henry K. Douglas, "Stonewall Jackson in Maryland," *Battles and Leaders of the Civil War*, Volume II. (New York: The Century Co., 1887-88).

**

While the Confederates were met with a general absence of cordiality in that part of Maryland, the troops did fare well during their stay in Frederick. "Supplies were plentiful; food and clothing were gratuitously distributed, and Jackson was presented with a fine but unbroken charger. The gift was timely, for 'Little Sorrel,' the companion of so many marches, was lost for some days after the passage of the Potomac; but the Confederacy was near paying a heavy price for the 'good grey mare.' When Jackson first mounted her, a band struck up close by, and as she reared the girth broke, throwing her rider to the ground. Fortunately, though stunned and severely bruised, the general was only temporarily disabled."

Col. G. F. R. Henderson, *Stonewall Jackson and the American Civil War.* Volume II. (London: Longmans, Green, & Co., 1900).

Thursday, September 11, 1862

George Shreve, an artilleryman in Stuart's Horse Artillery, wrote, "Genl. Lee issued strict orders against taking any property by the soldiers. Some of the men came into camp one morning with a pig, and declared that the pig attacked them, and they were obliged to kill it in self defense. It was keenly enjoyed for breakfast and no questions asked."

George W. Shreve, *Reminiscences in the History of the Stuart Horse Artillery, C.S.A.* (R. Preston Chew papers, Jefferson County Museum, Charles Town, West Virginia).

**

Mistrust and thievery abounded as both armies passed through the border state. Capt. James Oden (the quartermaster of the Fifth Virginia Cavalry) and a detachment of Confederate troopers visited the rural Maryland farm of three "strapping women," who were of Germanic descent. Seeing the enemy soldiers approaching, these sturdy ladies locked their front door, grabbed pitchforks, and marched to the front of their well stocked barn, where they turned to face the astonished Confederates. A quick-thinking Oden detailed a squad to go to the farmhouse and feign breaking in the front door. The trio of ladies raced towards their home, leveled their pitchforks, and charged the soldiers. Thus distracted, they had abandoned their intended defense of the barn and its livestock. Captain Oden and his other cavalrymen quickly entered the barn and gleefully rounded up four fine horses. The Rebels fled the scene, taking their prizes with them, while the ladies shrieked and cursed at them in excited German.

Ezra Carman, *The Maryland Campaign.* (Manuscript Division, Library of Congress).

**

      An alternative to blatantly stealing food and provisions was to simply ask. As the One Hundred and Twenty-fourth Pennsylvania hastily marched out, they had not taken time for breakfast or lunch, nor had they eaten supper the night before. The day was dreary and rainy, and the regiment finally slogged through the mud to the village of Damascus, where it halted for the night. Cpl. David Wilkinson and Pvt. Morgan Pinkerton, both wet and hungry, soon left the campsite and went foraging. Walking over to a distant old house, they knocked on the door and were soon welcomed inside by an aged couple. The owners obliged the tired boys in blue and soon set before them a veritable feast, replete with a large corn cake and boiled string beans and potatoes. The grateful lads dug into their haversacks and shared coffee and sugar with their hosts, and everyone had a good time conversing and dining. After the excellent meal, the soldiers presented the couple with a dollar in appreciation. They had eaten so much they could hardly make it back to their camp in the rain and darkness.

Robert M. Green, ed., *History of the One Hundred and Twenty-fourth Regiment Pennsylvania Volunteers.* (Philadelphia: Ware Bros. Company, 1907).

**

      As the One Hundred Thirty-second Pennsylvania camped near Frederick, a local farmer boldly walked past the guards and asked to see the colonel. Since Col. Richard Oakford and Lt. Col. Vincent Wilcox both were temporarily absent, the Marylander was ushered into the presence of Maj. Charles Albright, who had been left in charge of the regiment that evening. The enraged farmer insisted that "you 'uns" had stolen his last pig, and he demanded immediate payment. Albright, an experienced pre-war attorney, cross-examined the angry farmer, peppering him with questions to establish why he was so sure this particular regiment had committed the offense, as there were at least fifty other regiments in the vicinity during the timeframe of the pig snatching. The farmer would not be denied. He insisted that the culprits were "a hundred and thirty-two 'uns," as he had noted their cap insignia as they made off with the purloined pig. As it had not been very long since the incident, the farmer offered to search the camp and identify his pig.

      Major Albright was not through with his closing argument, however. He built a strong case that his men were greenhorns, totally unaccustomed to foraging, and that the real perpetrators could only have been seasoned veterans who had laid the blame on the rookie soldiers. So persuasive was Albright that the farmer finally departed, satisfied that he had accused the wrong regiment. He had not gone very far when the major's attention was distracted by the approach of one of his men, who presented him with a fine piece of fresh pork for his supper. Albright had sincerely believed his men were innocent and had skillfully defended them against their accuser, all while the scamps were behind the camp butchering and dressing the farmer's pig. According to the regimental adjutant, "how they managed to capture and kill that pig, without a single squeal escaping, is one of the marvels of the service." The staff officers, a chagrined Major Albright included, soon settled down to eat the evidence.

Frederick L. Hitchcock, *War From the Inside: The Story of the 132ⁿᵈ Regiment Pennsylvania Volunteer Infantry in the War for the Suppression of the Rebellion.* (Philadelphia: J. B. Lippincott, 1904).

**

Foraging in unfamiliar territory had definite hazards. As one portly Pennsylvania plunderer jerked a ripe apple from an overburdened branch, he inadvertently also knocked down a hornet's nest. Angered by their sudden fall, the hornets savagely attacked the soldier and nearly killed him before he could jump over the farmer's fence and race down the road in the twilight. By the time he had finally outdistanced the last of the swarm, he had been stung over an eye, in his nose, and several times in his scalp.

Archibald F. Hill, *Our Boys.* (Philadelphia: John E. Potter, 1864).

**

Capt. John Nance of the Third South Carolina wanted to impress the regimental colonel (his brother James) and Lt. Col. William Rutherford, who just happened to be engaged to his sister. Nance's foragers had scrounged up a nice-sized chicken, but, being too old to fry, it had to be stewed. Captain Nance ordered his black servant, Jess, to bake a batch of biscuits that night and safely stash them away until morning, when the chicken would be cooked and a fine breakfast spread presented to his guests. Jess obliged, and, by early evening, the biscuits were baked and piled high on an old tin plate. The servant quietly placed them in the captain's tent at his head for safekeeping and caught a few hours of sleep.

Rising quite early the next morning, Jess began to cook the fowl in an iron pan over the fire. As the teasing aroma of chicken stew wafted through the camp, the colonel and Nance's future brother-in-law were seated upon the ground, expectantly waiting the breakfast call. Some of Nance's enlisted men were a trifle jealous that, while the captain made merry with his guests eating chicken and biscuits, they would be munching on hardtack. They decided to play a prank on their captain, who was busy assisting Jess in putting the finishing touches to the tempting meal, as well as doing the honors to his distinguished guests.

When all was ready, Nance ordered Jess to bring out the biscuits, and the servant ducked into the captain's nearby tent. Several minutes passed, and still Jess did not reappear with the plate. Captain Nance, frustrated by his appetite and embarrassed in the presence of his superiors, angrily called out, "Why in the thunder don't you bring out the biscuits, Jess?" Inside Nance's little four-by-six tent, blankets were being frantically overturned and turned again and knapsacks moved for the fourth or fifth time, as Jess faithfully hunted for the missing plate of biscuits. An exasperated Nance soon thundered, "Why in the h——l don't you come on with the biscuits, Jess?" with a pronounced accent on the word "Jess." Finally, Jess poked his black, shaggy head through the tent door, the white of his eyes depicting the anguish of his mind and his voice betraying the despair he felt. He answered: "Well, Marse John, before God Almighty, ef somebody ain't tooken stole dem bisket." Nance and his guests had to eat their steaming stew without the bread.

The sequel to the biscuit story came twenty-five years later, well after the Civil War, at a big revival meeting at Bethel Church in Nance's native Newberry County, North Carolina. A great many "hard cases" were greatly impressed with the fire-and-brimstone sermons. One particular unrepentant man, John Mathis, especially seemed on the point of "getting religion," but he looked to be burdened with a great weight. At the end of the lengthy service, he sought out a now middle-aged Captain Nance and expressed a desire to make a confession. "Did you ever know who stole your biscuits that night at Frederick City?" "No." "Well, I and Bud Wilson—" But Nance never allowed Mathis to finish, for, as the light of that far-off truth dawned upon him and seemed to bring back the recollection of that nice brown chicken and the missing biscuits, he solemnly intoned, "No, I'll never forgive you; go home and don't try for religion any longer, for a crime as heinous as yours is beyond forgiveness. Oh, such depravity!"

D. Augustus Dickert, *History of Kershaw's Brigade*. (Newberry, SC: Elbert H. Aull Co., 1899).

Friday, September 12, 1862

Disease and enemy gunfire were the leading caused of death during the Civil War. Accidental deaths and friendly fire incidents were also somewhat common. However, in comparison, deaths caused by animals were rather scarce. Even as the Rebel rear guard left Frederick, the Union vanguard was arriving. One Confederate trooper was killed in the ensuing cavalry skirmish by a freak accident. One of the regiment's horses became unruly, and, running away, it struck the cord attached to the primer of a loaded cannon. The piece immediately discharged its contents of canister, killing a nearby Rebel cavalryman.

Richmond *Daily Dispatch*, September 22, 1862.

**

After the brief, but sharp skirmish in Frederick's streets, Wade Hampton's Confederate cavalry brigade rode out one end of the main street and Maj. Gen. Jacob D. Cox's Union infantry division marched in at the other. Even as carbine smoke and the smell of expended gunpowder lingered in the air, closed window shutters flew open, sashes went up, and the windows were filled with ladies waving handkerchiefs and national flags. Several women emerged beside the street to hand out fruit and refreshments for the soldiers as they marched by in the hot afternoon sunshine. Cox and his men never forgot the kindness of Frederick's ladies.

Jacob D. Cox, *Military Reminiscences of the Civil War, Vol. I.* (New York: Charles Scribner's Sons, 1900).

**

  As elements of Lee's advancing army passed through Funkstown, Maryland, one charitable resident, Angela Davis, set out buckets of cold water by her front door, along with several tin cups for the passing troops to quench their thirst. Although she had been born in New York and was decidedly pro-Union, she felt it was her Christian duty to give a cup of cold water to her enemies. Occasionally, wary Rebels asked her to sample the water first, fearing that the woman may have poisoned it. As she was conversing with some soldiers, a dusty officer rode up and demanded a cup of water from one of the enlisted men. As he lifted the tin cup to his superior, the private innocently remarked, "A Yankee lady is giving us the water." The secessionist officer, aghast that he was accepting water from a Northern sympathizer, angrily flung the cup to the ground and disgustedly remarked, "If that is so, then I will not drink a drop of it!" With an air of arrogance, he spurred his horse and rode off, leaving the embarrassed soldiers standing there with a stunned Mrs. Davis. One tried to soothe her by claiming the officer must have been drunk, and not to let his rudeness bother her. Undaunted, Davis continued her generosity.

Angela Kirkham Davis, *War Recollections.* (Files of the Antietam National Battlefield).

**

  In many other Maryland locales, the reception for the Rebels was as chilly as the well water. As Stonewall Jackson and his staff rode along, Lt. Henry Kyd Douglas noted, "In Middletown two very pretty girls, with ribbons of red, white, and blue floating from their hair, and small Union flags in their hands, rushed out of a house as we passed, came to the curbstone, and with much laughter waved their flags defiantly in the face of the general. He bowed and raised his hat, and, turning with his quiet smile to his staff, said: 'We evidently have no friends in this town.'"

Henry K. Douglas, "Stonewall Jackson in Maryland," *Battles and Leaders of the Civil War*, Volume II. (New York: The Century Co., 1887-88).

**

  While at Frederick, Robert E. Lee had devised a daring plan to capture the Federal garrison at Harper's Ferry, Virginia. He had split the Army of Northern Virginia into several segments, with the intent of surrounding Harper's Ferry with three columns, including that of Stonewall Jackson. He also needed to protect his flanks by denying easy Federal access across the sprawling South Mountain range just to the northeast. Joseph Kershaw's South Carolina brigade spent much of Friday ascending the towering Elk Ridge to get into position to seize its prominent southern tip, Maryland Heights, control of which would decide the fate of Harper's Ferry. Kershaw's sweating and cursing men had to pull themselves up precipitous inclines by the twigs and undergrowth that lined the 1,400-foot-high mountainside, or hold themselves in position by the trees in front while they searched for a safe foothold to climb higher. Cuts and scrapes abounded as men slid part way back down the rocky bramble-covered slope before recovering and finally reaching the crest.

At night, the exhausted men bivouacked on the mountain. They could see campfires all along the slopes and gorges through Pleasant Valley and up on neighboring South Mountain, where the Georgia troops of Ambrose Wright had camped opposite. Concurrently, over 13,000 Federals peacefully slumbered at Harper's Ferry, most unaware that they were being slowly surrounded by Stonewall.

D. Augustus Dickert, *History of Kershaw's Brigade*. (Newberry, SC: Elbert H. Aull Co., 1899).

**

After the war, Col. Clement Evans of the Thirty-first Georgia wrote a vivid description that captures the image of the majority of Lee's army during the Maryland Campaign. "It is difficult to describe the condition of the troops at this time, so great and various was their wretchedness. They were sunburnt, gaunt, ragged, scarcely at all shod – specters and caricatures of their former selves. Since the beginning of August they had been almost constantly on the march, had been scorched by the sultriest sun of the year, had been drenched with the rain and the heavy dews peculiar to this latitude, had lost much night rest, had worn out their clothing and shoes, and received nothing but what they could pick up on the battlefield. They had thrown away their knapsacks and blankets, in order to travel light; had fed on half-cooked dough, often raw bacon as well as raw beef; had devoured green corn and green apples, and contracted diarrhea and dysentery of the most malignant type. They now stood, an emaciated, limping, ragged mass, whom no stranger to their gallant exploits could have believed capable of anything the least worthy."

Clement A. Evans, ed., *Confederate Military History*. (Atlanta: Confederate Publishing Company, 1899).

**

In stark contrast to the "ragged Rebels," a number of Federal regiments looked as if they were fresh off the parade ground. Recuperating from Second Bull Run at Fairfax Court House, Virginia, the Forty-eighth Pennsylvania had been issued brand new uniforms, the first they had worn since they had originally enlisted. The tattered and threadbare dirty old clothing, filled with vermin, was quickly cast aside for the crisp look of the new woolen uniforms. Their knapsacks and extraneous accoutrements had been left behind on the battlefield at Manassas and subsequently lost, but now the Pennsylvanians received new dog tents and equipment. They were in fine appearance and well supplied as they marched into Maryland. Upon their arrival in Frederick, they were greeted with brightly illuminated houses and enthusiastic residents proudly waving flags and banners and singing patriotic songs. Food and refreshment abounded for the soldiers, and their corps commander, Maj. Gen. Ambrose Burnside, had his passage through town blocked by jubilant citizens eager to "thank and bless him as their deliverer." Ladies crowded about Burnside and kissed his hands, while others up in the balconies of private residences rained bouquets down upon the celebrated general.

Joseph Gould, *The Story of the Forty-eighth: a Record of the Campaigns of the Forty-eighth Regiment Pennsylvania Veteran Volunteer Infantry...* (Alfred M. Slocum Co., 1908)

**

Many Union regiments received the same lavish welcome as they paraded through Frederick on September 12. The One Hundred and Sixth Pennsylvania had endured a trying march, cutting across fields, meadows, fences, fresh plowed ground, cornfields, and woods, all because the roads were clogged with artillery and cavalry. Hot, tired, and dirty, they camped for the night near Urbana, Maryland and refreshed themselves as much as possible. As they tramped into Frederick the following day, they received a "royal and patriotic welcome," as, seemingly, the entire population turned out to greet the passing army. Cheering citizens passed out ice water and cold milk, and women and children pressed cakes, pies, and bread into the eager hands of the grateful soldiers as they marched by. Handkerchiefs and flags abounded, and the festivities continued throughout the grand procession through town. General McClellan had passed by the regiment at one point and entered Frederick, and "the people were almost wild; they blocked the streets, almost covering him and his horse with flags, as many as could shaking him by the hand, and all cheering him as long as he was in sight."

Joseph R. C. Ward, *History of the One Hundred and Sixth Regiment, Pennsylvania Volunteers.* (Philadelphia: Grant, Faires, & Rodgers, 1883).

**

Food was on the mind of soldiers from both armies. General Lee had issued strict orders to the Army of Northern Virginia against pilfering from private property. Likewise, a number of similar orders circulated among the Army of the Potomac. As the Nineteenth Massachusetts settled into camp on the outskirts of Frederick, the regimental adjutant read the perfunctory order banning foraging. While the officer droned on, Lt. James Reynolds noticed his black servant, Henry Johnson, walking into the camp with a pair of stoneware crocks, one neatly tucked under each arm. The officers of Company D quickly flashed signals to Johnson to hide the contraband, and, grinning at them, he ducked into cover before the regimental staff could see him with his prize, which turned out to be fresh butter. Reynolds and his fellow officers "managed to make good use of the butter. It was too much of a luxury to part with, orders or no orders."

Ernst Linden Waitt, *History of the Nineteenth Regiment Massachusetts Volunteer Infantry 1861-1865.* (Salem, Massachusetts: Salem Press, 1906).

Saturday, September 13, 1862

During the morning, Stonewall Jackson arrived in Martinsburg, Virginia, on his march to seize Harper's Ferry. "Here the general was welcomed with enthusiasm, and a great crowd hastened to the hotel to greet him. At first he shut himself up in a room to write dispatches, but the demonstration became so persistent that he ordered the door to be opened. The crowd, chiefly ladies, rushed in and embarrassed the general with every possible outburst of affection, to which he could only reply, 'Thank you, you are very kind.' He gave them his autograph in books and on scraps of paper, cut a button from his coat for a little girl, and then submitted patiently to an attack by the others, who soon stripped the coat of nearly all the remaining buttons. But when they looked beseechingly at his hair, which was thin, he drew the line, and managed to close the interview." The ladies of Martinsburg made such desperate assaults on the mane and tail of the general's charger that he had at last to post a sentry over the stable. By the afternoon, he and his men had moved on.

Col. G. F. R. Henderson, *Stonewall Jackson and the American Civil War.* Volume II. (London: Longmans, Green, & Co., 1900).

**

Company F of the Twenty-seventh Indiana, part of the Federal XII Corps, had advanced westward in the morning as a skirmish line towards Frederick, but had been ordered aside to allow the passage of the IX Corps. Relaxing under a clump of trees in a clover field on the David Best farm not far from the Georgetown Pike, Sgt. John Bloss, Cpl. Barton W. Mitchell, and Pvt. David Vance were enjoying the respite and conversing. Unexpectedly spotting a long yellow envelope in the grass, a curious Vance picked it up, and, to his surprise, noted that it was addressed to Gen. D. H. Hill, who commanded a division in the Confederate army. As the envelope was passed to the sergeant, out fell a piece of paper wrapped around three cigars. As the excited Hoosiers smoked one of their new finds, they read the note, which turned out to be a copy of Robert E. Lee's specific orders outlining the routes of march for the widely scattered Confederate army. The note, written four days earlier, was soon routed up the chain of command to General McClellan, who realized that, if he could strike quickly, he might be able to crush Lee's army. Holding the two-page letter, McClellan exclaimed, "Here is a paper with which, if I cannot whip Bobby Lee, I will be willing to go home."

Files of the Antietam National Battlefield, National Park Service.

**

The Fourteenth Connecticut was nicknamed the "Nutmegs," a sobriquet for men from that state where the tasty spice was commonplace. Ground or grated, nutmeg was considered a delicacy. On Saturday, the regiment marched into Frederick and passed by an old fire engine house where several Confederate prisoners of war were being held. One plucky Rebel called out, wanting to know what regiment the Yankees were from.

"The Fourteenth Wooden Nutmegs," proudly replied the passing column. An audacious prisoner wryly responded, "You will soon get your heads grated."

Charles Davis Page, *History of the Fourteenth Regiment, Connecticut Vol. Infantry.* (Meriden: Horton Print. Co., 1906).

**

The Union IX Corps passed a house belonging to a branch of the family of George Washington. A few officers of the Kanawha Division accompanied their commander, Maj. Gen. Jacob Cox, at the invitation of the occupant, to look at some relics of the "Father of his Country" that had been preserved there. The officers stood for some minutes with uncovered heads before a display case containing a uniform General Washington had worn in the Continental Army, as well as other articles of personal use hallowed by their association with him. Cox and his subordinates went on their way with their "zeal strengthened by closer contact with souvenirs of the great patriot."

Jacob D. Cox, *Military Reminiscences of the Civil War, Vol. I.* (New York: Charles Scribner's Sons, 1900).

**

One Federal regiment marching through Maryland had a chance to perform a civic duty for the residents of Frederick. Shortly before noon, rioting inmates in the Frederick County Jail set fire to the building, hoping to escape in the confusion. The county sheriff, Michael Zimmerman, ignored the prisoners and began hauling his office furniture out into the street. Two stragglers from the Ninth New York (the "Hawkins Zouaves") were in the vicinity, having conveniently missed going out on patrol to nearby Jefferson, Maryland. Exploring the town, they noticed flames shooting from the roof of the building and raced over to help. Lt. James Horner helped the sheriff drag out the remaining furnishings, while Capt. William G. Barnett quickly ran back to the regiment's campsite and encountered Lt. Col. Edgar Kimball, who had just led the Ninth New York back from its patrol.

The veteran Zouaves, exhausted from their 25 mile march, had just bedded down in a grassy field to get some much needed rest when Barnett arrived with the tale of the burning jail. Kimball ordered three companies to arise and follow the captain to assist. The sleepy men piled out of their blankets and ran back with Barnett to the jail, where they helped Sheriff Zimmerman and Lieutenant Horner open the cell doors and shepherd the gagging prisoners outside to fresh air in the jail yard. Captain Barnett placed sentries around the yard to prevent anyone from escaping, while one detachment tried vainly to arrest the fire, which by now was fully consuming the wooden interior of the old stone jailhouse.

Matthew J. Graham, *The Ninth Regiment New York Volunteers (Hawkins' Zouaves)...* (New York: E. P. Copy & Co., 1900).

**

One of David Thompson's tent-mates in the Ninth New York was an enterprising young fellow. After the regiment had returned to Frederick from its tiring expedition to Jefferson, he embarked on a late night foraging mission. Sick and tired of the monotonous daily regimen of hard tack and "salt horse" (dried beef), he had vowed to break the routine. Now was his chance in the darkness and bustle as the regiment settled down for a short rest. He slipped into the night and was gone. Soon, the soldier returned, struggling with the weight of considerable plunder. He had purloined a crock of butter, a large quantity of apple butter, some lard, a three-legged iron skillet weighing several pounds, and a live hen. Thompson marveled at how the man managed to carry so much, but he was an experienced forager, with a comprehensive method that thoroughly covered the area. That night, Company G enjoyed several immense flapjacks, each the whole size of the pan. Tethering the captive hen to one of the tent pegs, they all went to sleep, only to be roused an hour or so later by hearing their two-legged prize cackling and fluttering off in the darkness.

David L. Thompson, "In the Ranks to the Antietam," *Battles and Leaders of the Civil War*, Volume II. (New York: The Century Co., 1887-88).

**

As the One Hundred and Twenty-fourth Pennsylvania paused at Frederick for a few hours of much needed rest, Cpl. Joel Hollingsworth took a squad from Company D to scavenge straw and fence rails to make beds. One of his soldiers, a man named Jack, spotted a straw rick on top of a nearby hill. He panted his way to the top and soon had collected two large bundles of straw. He descended and was almost back to camp when he happened to encounter division commander Maj. Gen. George Meade and his staff. Meade, who had issued strict orders against foraging, inquired, "Young man, where did you get that straw?" Jack gestured, "Up there on the hill." A frowning Meade sternly ordered, "Well, you take it back." Jack retorted, "General, I suppose I will have to obey your order, but if you were not wearing shoulder straps, I'll be d____ if I would." The combative Meade dismounted, angrily pulled off his general's coat, and threw it onto his saddle. He turned to the enlisted man and challenged, "Now, young man, the straps are out of the way; you take the straw back." Jack, unwilling to fight with a general, sullenly made two trips to carry the straw back up the steep hillside, cursing Meade all the way.

Robert M. Green, ed., *History of the One Hundred and Twenty-fourth Regiment Pennsylvania Volunteers.* (Philadelphia: Ware Bros. Company, 1907).

**

Samuel Garland, Jr. was an excellent Confederate general who has been long forgotten by the general public, perhaps due to his untimely death at South Mountain during the Maryland Campaign. A grand-nephew of former President James Madison, Garland had suffered through the loss of his beloved wife in June 1861 and, three months later, his infant son Samuel also died. General Garland became known for his fearlessness under fire, so much so that rumors abounded he had a death wish. However, his men admired and remembered him forever for the compassion and thoughtfulness that he typically demonstrated towards them. As his North Carolina brigade was crossing one Maryland creek on a narrow footway, many of his men impatiently began to plunge into the little stream, wading in water up to their knees. Garland knew it would be bad for them to march with wet feet. He drew up his fiery horse in the road in the water and stayed there till his entire command had passed, pointing to the narrow bridge and shouting to the men, compelling them to take their time and go over in single file.

Rev. Alexander D. Betts, *Experience of a Confederate Chaplain, 1861-1864.* (Greenville, South Carolina: 1900s). University of North Carolina library, Call number C970.78 B56e.

**

     In the shadows of imposing South Mountain, Federal and Confederate cavalry clashed between Middletown and Burkittsville on the grounds of a small old-fashioned country schoolhouse. School was in session and, as Union cavalry formed in a meadow by the Quebec School, the teacher "cast a wistful look" outward from the open door at the troopers. Soon, three open windows were filled with curious students jostling for a better glimpse of the blue-clad cavalrymen and their fully equipped mounts. Occasionally, two or three small children would peer out the door from behind the teacher's coattails. The soldiers from distant Illinois and Indiana stared back. Ironically, half of Company F of the Third Indiana Cavalry, including Cpl. William N. Pickerill, had been country schoolteachers before they enlisted.

     The pastoral scene, the innocent faces of the wide-eyed children, the one-room whitewashed country school – all elicited memories of home for the Hoosiers. "Although we were equipped for war, it seemed for the moment like old times, old friends and the old schoolhouse of our far off western homes again. For the moment we were on furlough from the turmoil and anxiety of war, back in the old home schoolhouse, with its playgrounds and romping with the boys and girls who had been the playmates of our childhood." Pickerill's dreamy reverie was soon shattered. Wade Hampton's Cobb Legion cavalry suddenly emerged from the nearby woods and savagely attacked the Federals "with drawn swords, wild-eyed, cursing us furiously and demanding our surrender." Some thirty or forty opposing troopers fell in the ensuing skirmish, while the teacher and his students huddled in the wooden schoolhouse. After the firing ceased and the last of the cavalrymen had departed, school was finally dismissed and the students and teacher hastened home, full of tales of the fight at Quebec School.

Middletown *Valley Register*, April 8, 1898.

**

     Unlike northern Virginia, the farmlands of Maryland were unscarred by war, and opportunities abounded for the soldiers to procure (legally or otherwise) food, delicacies, clothing, and other pleasures. After the Seventeenth Michigan paused for the night after a hard day's march, Lt. Christian Rath was hungry. His men were stacking their muskets when Rath suddenly asked, "Where's John Coneley?" No one knew for sure, although it was strongly suspected that he had fallen out of the ranks for a private foraging expedition. Not to be deterred, the lieutenant demanded, "Well, then send me the next best thief; I want a chicken for supper." A number of soldiers headed to a nearby farm and procured the officer's desired fowl, as well as gathering fresh fruit. Rath and his men ate well that Saturday night at the expense of the Maryland farmer.

David G. Lane, *A Soldier's Diary.* (privately printed, 1905).

**

That same evening, the Twenty-first Massachusetts, hungry and dusty, marched into Middletown, Maryland, in bright moonlight. They were greeted by the ghoulish sight of two dead Rebels swinging from stout ropes attached to a large tree. Residents soon informed the soldiers that these Confederates had been executed by their own provost guard for stealing apples from a nearby orchard, apparently in compliance with an order from General Lee. Undaunted, the famished Yankees left the two rotting enemy corpses dangling, and then proceeded to raid every chicken coop and pig pen they could find. They even pilfered most of the fruit from the same apple orchard that the "Johnnies" had visited in their last moments on earth. Unlike the Southerners, no punishment came to the Massachusetts boys for their wanton thievery.

Charles F. Walcott, *History of the 21st Massachusetts Volunteers in the War for the Preservation of the Union.* (Boston: Houghton, Mifflin & Co., 1882).

Chapter 2

South Mountain
and Harper's Ferry

South Mountain is an imposing ridgeline running from Pennsylvania southward through central Maryland. An extension of the Blue Ridge Mountains, much of South Mountain is over 1,000 feet in elevation, and, during the Civil War, it formed a solid barrier against the movement of troops across its steep slopes. North of the Potomac River, the mountains were passable via a few gaps or lower areas. As Lee concentrated his army west of South Mountain near Sharpsburg, he positioned various strong detachments to guard four of the most likely gaps that the pursuing Federal army might use. From south to north, these were Brownsville Gap, Crampton's Gap (near Burkittsville), Fox's Gap, and Turner's Gap. The latter, a 600-foot-high pass between two 1,000-foot peaks, was traversed by the National Road, one of the first roads to go from the East Coast into the western wilderness – the Ohio Country.

Union commander George McClellan ordered Maj. Gen. William Franklin's VI Corps to seize Crampton's Gap, while Generals Jesse Reno (IX Corps) and Joseph Hooker (I Corps) were to take Fox's and Turner's Gaps. Confederate Maj. Gen. D. H. Hill was charged with defending the vital passes, buying enough time for Stonewall Jackson to surround and capture the Federal base at nearby Harper's Ferry.

Sunday, September 14, 1862

The Ninth Virginia Cavalry was a part of the brigade commanded by Brig. Gen. Fitz Lee, a nephew of Robert E. Lee. One of the troopers later wrote, "After nine days spent among the fine hay and rich yellow cornfields of Montgomery and Frederick counties, the regiment crossed the Catoctin mountain at Hamburg, at dawn on the 14th. Hamburg was a rude and scattering village on the crest of the mountain, where the manufacture of brandy seemed to be the chief employment of the villagers, and at the early hour of our passage through the place, both the men and women gave proof that they were free imbibers of the product of their stills, and it was not easy to find a sober inhabitant of either sex." Apparently Saturday night was party night in Hamburg, and the effects of the heavy drinking had carried through to Sunday morning.

"The Cavalry Fight At Boonsboro' Graphically Described," *Southern Historical Society Papers*, Vol. XXV Maryland Campaign. (Richmond, Virginia: January-December 1897).

**

Honor was still common among many soldiers, particularly among officers and gentlemen who believed that their word was a sacred trust. Sunday had dawned crisp and bright. Major General Cox accompanied Col. Eliakim Scammon's brigade on a reconnaissance. Just as the two officers crossed the meandering Catoctin Creek, they were surprised to see the familiar figure of Col. Augustus Moor of the Twenty-eighth Ohio standing alongside the dusty road. The 49-year-old Moor had been captured by Confederates during an earlier skirmish and Cox had assumed his former subordinate had been sent to captivity in the South. Such was not the case. An astonished Cox inquired as to how Moor had happened to be standing there, alone and without arms, sword, or horse.

Colonel Moor replied that he had been taken beyond South Mountain after being captured, but had been paroled the night before. He had decided to walk across the mountain pass and head east on the National Road, hoping to run into the Union army. Ironically, the first Federal he encountered was his own commanding general. Probably equally surprised to see the major general well in front of a single brigade, he asked Cox, "But where are you going?" Cox replied that Scammon was going to support the Federal cavalry in a reconnaissance of Turner's Gap up on South Mountain. Involuntarily, a startled Moor replied, "My God! Be Careful!" Catching himself, he added, "But I am paroled!" and turned away, refusing to reveal the strength and disposition of the Confederate troops per his parole agreement.

Honor and honesty was more important to the German-born Moor than assisting his commander in preparing for battle. However, Cox, now having at least some foreshadowing that serious danger lurked in the distant mountain pass, rode back along the column and spoke to each regimental commander, warning them to be prepared for anything, big or little – they might be facing a mere skirmish, or it might be a major battle. Taking no chances, and correctly reading in Moor's countenance the seriousness of the Rebel opposition, Cox sent a message to the IX Corps commander, Jesse Reno, that he was sending in the rest of his division to support Scammon. It would prove to be a wise decision. Had the Confederates not released Colonel Moor, Cox may not have known what was in front of his recon patrol.

Jacob D. Cox, *Military Reminiscences of the Civil War, Vol. I.* (New York: Charles Scribner's Sons, 1900).

**

As the Union I Corps passed through Middletown and deployed for their assault on Turner's Gap, an admiring George Kimball of the Twelfth Massachusetts noticed Major General McClellan sitting upon his horse in the road. McClellan had recently been restored to command, and many of his men adored "Little Mac." About a mile or two beyond the regiment's position were the Rebels, high up on the slopes of South Mountain guarding Turner's Gap and nearby Fox's Gap. The divisions of John Hatch and Jesse Reno were already in action, and a cloud of white gunsmoke lingered halfway up the mountainside. As they listened to the rumble of the guns, none of the soldiers were certain what the future held. However as each regiment in turn passed McClellan, the men became forgetful of everything but their intense love for him. They cheered and cheered again, until they became so hoarse they could shout no longer.

According to Kimball, "It seemed as if an intermission had been declared in order that a reception might be tendered to the general-in-chief. A great crowd continually surrounded him, and the most extravagant demonstrations were indulged in.

30

Hundreds even hugged the horse's legs and caressed his head and mane. While the troops were thus surging by, the general continually pointed with his finger to the gap in the mountain though which our path lay." Ahead was possible injury or death, but, for now, the soldiers eagerly wanted to please their leader.

R. U. Johnson and C. C. Buel, *Battles and Leaders of the Civil War*, Volume II. (New York: The Century Co., 1887-88).

**

Maj. Gen. D. H. Hill commanded most of the Confederates on South Mountain. In the morning, he and his aide, Maj. John Ratchford, rode from Turner's Gap using a rude lane used to haul wood, intending to inspect the position of a nearby Georgia brigade posted just to the south. On their way back, they paused at the isolated wooden cabin of P. Hartley, which stood in a small clearing along the western side of the old road. Hartley and his three small children were still at home, unaware until the armies arrived that a battle was imminent. Standing in his front yard, Hartley was met by Ratchford, who inquired as to what the mountaineer knew about the positions of nearby Federal artillery. Since the major was wearing an old Federal blue greatcoat he had captured at Seven Pines during the Peninsular Campaign earlier in the year, Hartley believed him to be a lost Yankee and retorted, "The road in which your battery is on comes into the valley road near the church."

Ratchford and Hill soon realized that the farmer did not know who they really were, so they played along like they were indeed Federals and began asking questions about the Rebel troop strength. Hill, perhaps suppressing a smile, casually inquired, "Who is in command?" A man fond of his own reputation, the general must have been taken aback when Hartley replied, "I don't know," and shrugged as if he really didn't even care. About that time, a Union artillery shell crashed through the trees above their heads and one of Hartley's daughters shrieked in terror. Hill comforted her as much as he could, and then spurred his horse to join Ratchford on the ride northward toward his headquarters in Turner's Gap.

R. U. Johnson and C. C. Buel, *Battles and Leaders of the Civil War*, Volume II. (New York: The Century Co., 1887-88).

**

Hill and Ratchford were not the only soldiers questioning local civilians about the whereabouts of the enemy. As the long Federal lines deployed in the scenic valley below South Mountain, Confederate artillery batteries tried to depress their muzzles far enough to lob shells at the approaching lines of Union infantry. In most cases, these shells harmlessly hurled over the Union troops and landed in their rear. Undeterred, the battle lines slowly walked forward with parade ground precision, with officers on horseback flashing bright swords, and then began ascending the mountain slopes. As the Seventy-sixth New York began its advance, the infantrymen noted three local women who came down the side of the mountain on horseback by a diagonal path and passed in front of the small regiment. The regimental color bearer, Charles E. Stamp, addressed them and inquired about the Confederate forces on top of the mountain. They were the

31

last women the blue-eyed handsome youth would ever see. Less than half an hour later, Sergeant Stamp was dead from a bullet wound in his forehead, one of hundreds of victims of the Battle of South Mountain.

Uberto A. Burnham, "South Mountain – Maryland Campaign," *The National Tribune,* 1928.

**

Dozens of men would later write of the panoramic view from the slopes of South Mountain looking eastward. Capt. George Noyes, the aide-de-camp to Brig. Gen. Abner Doubleday, later penned that "stretching off toward the north and east is a lovely swale, buttressed by hilly ranges, smiling with orchards, fields of ripening grain, and cheerful farm-houses—truly a valley of content and beauty. There is little of the sublime about this view, but it is very soothing, and offers so strong a contrast to our present fearful business as to daguerreotype itself upon my imagination forever…"

"'What a magnificent view!' exclaims the general, as he turns in his saddle to inspect his brigade, and catches one glance of the beautiful panorama. A moment's breathing period, and he orders the brigade to march by the flank into the woods on our right, where, facing to the front, we move up at double-quick to meet the enemy. The little twigs above us, splintered and cut by the bullets, are cracking and falling about our heads; here and there a coward or two comes skulking out from the fight, a wounded brave limps past or lies half exhausted at the foot of a protecting tree. Yonder, behind a hickory, crouches one in the uniform of an officer—shame on his cowardice and evil example; on the instant his name and regiment are demanded, and he is driven back to his duty, perhaps, so singular is human nature, to fight bravely through the rest of the battle."

George F. Noyes, *The Bivouac and the Battle-Field; or, Campaign Sketches in Virginia and Maryland* (New York: Harper & Brothers, 1863)

**

Dodging death or injury was often a matter of luck, as well as the circumstances of the shot. While marching in a column of fours on South Mountain to their assigned position at Turner's Gap, the First Virginia came under some errant long-range Yankee artillery fire. A spent six-pound solid shot struck Pvt. John H. Daniel on his rump, hurling him ten feet, but not seriously injuring him. He would nurse a badly bruised butt for days.

Charles T. Loehr, *War History of the Old First Virginia Infantry Regiment, Army of Northern Virginia.* (Richmond: Wm. Ellis Jones, 1884).

**

The Confederates held a strong position protecting Turner's Gap with infantry in several key locations on the heights. The Federal soldiers were compelled to carry the seemingly impregnable position by direct assault. One group of Rebels occupied a ledge on the extreme right, unseen to the Union attackers. They unleashed a volley at Col. Hugh W. McNeil and a small contingent of the Thirteenth Pennsylvania Reserves of the I Corps. McNeil instantly commanded, "Pour your fire upon those rocks!" His men hesitated, as they were not accustomed to receive a collective order, as they had always picked their individual targets. "Fire!" thundered the colonel; "I tell you to fire on those rocks!" The men obeyed, spraying balls at the unseen foe up the mountainside.

For some time an irregular fire was kept up, with the Bucktails (so named for the deer tails worn in their hats) sheltering themselves as best they could behind trees and rocks. McNeil finally caught sight of two Rebs peering through an opening in the impromptu works, getting ready to aim. The eyes of the men followed their commander and half a dozen breech-loading rifles were leveled in that direction.

"Wait a minute," said the colonel, "I will try my hand. There is nothing like killing two birds with one stone." The two Confederates were not in straight line, but one stood a little distance back of the other, while just in front of the foremost was a slanting rock. Colonel McNeil seized a rifle, raised it, glanced a moment along the polished barrel; a loud report followed, and both Rebels disappeared. At that moment, a loud cheer from the rear lines rent the air. "All is right now," cried McNeil; "Charge the rascals!"

The men sprang up among the rocks in an instant. The Confederates turned to run, but encountered another detachment of the Bucktails and were obliged to surrender. Not a man of them escaped. Everyone then finally saw the object of the colonel's order to fire randomly among the rocks. He had sent a party around to the rear and used the random fire from downhill to attract their attention. It was a perfect success. The two Rebels by the opening in the ledge were found lying there stiff and cold. McNeil's bullet had struck the slanting rock in front of them, glanced off, and had amazingly passed through both their heads. There the lump of lead lay beside them, flattened. McNeil picked it up and put it in his pocket as a souvenir of South Mountain.

Hugh McNeil was still carrying the "lucky" bullet a few days later when he was killed at Antietam.

Frank Moore, *Anecdotes, Poetry, and Incidents of the War: North and South.* 1860-1865. (New York: Publication office, Bible house, J. Porteus, agent, 1867).

**

War can produce strange emotions within men, even among the most veteran of warriors. Within the Second Pennsylvania Reserves was an older soldier who had been through the Mexican-American War, as well as the Civil War to date. Despite his years of army service, amazingly, he had never actually been in a battle, as he was always shirking in the rear during combat. Neither the threats of his officers or ridicule of his fellow soldiers could induce him to go into danger, as he frequently declared he had a strong presentiment when he was a boy that he would be killed in the first fight he went into. However, some of his current comrades were determined that he should go into this battle and threatened to shoot him if he did not. The Second began its ascent of South Mountain towards Turner's Gap, with the shirker initially keeping up with his company.

Soon after the regiment came under Confederate fire, true to his character, the coward lay down behind the thick trunk of a tree, where he was perfectly safe and could ride out the battle. However, seeing a large rock a few feet from him, and, believing it offered even more protection, he anxiously got up to run to it. The very instant he rose, he fell dead with nine of the enemy's balls in him. His boyhood premonition had indeed finally come true.

E. M. Woodward, *Our Campaigns: The Second Regiment Pennsylvania Reserve Volunteers.* (Philadelphia: John E. Potter, 1865).

**

Life and death on the battlefield often was a matter of circumstance and timing. A Confederate regiment advanced towards a cornfield near Turner's Gap, unknowingly at an oblique angle to the hidden men of the Eighty-ninth New York Infantry, who were flat on their faces among the cornstalks. Neither side was initially aware of the other's presence. Finally discovering the prone Yankees, the Confederates stood before them, not twenty feet away, the full intention of destruction on their faces. However, they were helpless, as they were all carrying empty muskets. The New Yorkers simply rose up and shot them down.

David L. Thompson, "In the Ranks to the Antietam," *Battles and Leaders of the Civil War*, Volume II. (New York: The Century Co., 1887-88).

**

The color bearer of the Seventy-sixth New York, 21-year-old Charles Stamp, ran ahead of his regiment and planted his colors on a stone wall not far from Turner's Gap. Turning around to hustle on his comrades, he yelled, "There, come up to that!" Seconds later, a bullet ended his life on earth. The bloodied banner fluttered into the arms of Lt. James Goddard, who passionately called out, "Who is the next brave who dare take these colors?" "I am the boy," was heard above the din of battle, and Earl Evens, a light-haired, blue-eyed 19-year-old, grasped the flagstaff and waved the colors defiantly in the face of the enemy. Young Evens would have more luck than Stamp, safely carrying the colors through Antietam and many other battles, and surviving the war as a captain.

Cherry Valley (NY) *Gazette*, November 12, 1862. Abram P. Smith, *History of the Seventy-sixth Regiment New York Volunteers.* (Syracuse: Truair, Smith & Miles, 1867).

**

As the dismounted colonel of the Twenty-third Ohio urged his regiment up the forested slope towards Fox's Gap, he was struck by a bullet that shattered his left arm just above the elbow. Jolted by the unexpected blow, he somehow kept his feet and his composure, even as blood gushed from the open wound. He called out for an enlisted man to make a tourniquet with his handkerchief to stop the incessant flow, and continued to bark orders to his struggling men. Weakened by blood loss and shock, the colonel finally had to lie down to regain some strength. However, he refused to give up command of his regiment. Noting that some of his men were beginning to retire from a stone wall they held, he painfully staggered to his feet.

Using his sword as a cane, the wounded officer accosted a sergeant who was heading for the rear. "I am played out," the coward begged, "Please, sir, leave me alone." The irate colonel pointed to his bloody arm and snapped, "Look at *this*! Don't talk about being played out." Pointing to the stone wall, he angrily ordered, "*There* is your place in line!" Shamed by the stinging words, the noncom reluctantly rejoined the regiment at the wall. The Buckeye colonel, faint from the exertion, again lay down to rest. He survived his serious wound, became a brigadier general later in the war, and later served as the Nineteenth President of the United States – Rutherford B. Hayes.

Ezra Carman, "The Battle of South Mountain." Files of the Antietam National Battlefield, National Park Service.

**

Sometimes in the fog of war, a perceived threat can be just as terrifying as a real one. As the Sixteenth New York charged up the base of South Mountain through a dense cornfield towards a distant stone wall, the command "Right Oblique!" rang out. The regiment instantly responded, changing facing and moving ahead, except for privates James Allen and Darius Richards, who failed to hear the order. The duo blindly continued their advance to the stone wall, ignorant of the fact that they were now alone. As they drew near, they were met with a sudden volley that brought them to a halt as they ducked. Richards spoke first, "Hold on, Jim, what shall we do?" The 19-year-old Allen responded, "We'll charge them from behind that wall." As they rapidly advanced, the Rebels abandoned their breastworks and scooted up the steep mountainside. Richards was soon incapacitated by a bullet in the left leg as the pair climbed over the old stonewall. Allen found a comfortable place in a safe crevice to deposit his mate and made him comfortable, promising, "Richards, if I pull through all right, I'll come and take care of you." With that pledge, Allen doggedly picked his way alone up the brush-covered slope towards Crampton's Gap.

By that time, the Rebels had reached another stonewall lining a dirt road skirting the mountain. They ducked out of Allen's sight and disappeared beyond the rocks. Undaunted, young Allen climbed over the wall and was quickly met with another volley, which slightly wounded him. Thinking quickly, he put on a bold face and frantically waved his arms, screaming to his imaginary company, "Up men, up!" He then ordered the Confederates to surrender. Falling for the ruse and thinking they were cornered and outnumbered; the Rebels sullenly stacked their arms and raised their hands. The audacious Allen swiftly positioned himself between the men and their guns, and found that he had single-handedly taken fourteen prisoners and a stand of colors.

Just then, the commander of the Sixteenth New York, Lt. Col. Joel Seaver, rode up the road, halted just outside of musket range, and cautiously scanned the distant group through his field glasses. Spotting the Federal soldier and his party of unarmed prisoners, Seaver approached Allen and asked for details of how he had seized the fourteen Rebs. As Allen later carried the captured battle flag to his regiment, he was greeted with three hearty cheers. A detachment soon traipsed back down the mountain to retrieve the wounded Richards. For his valiant efforts, the Irish-born Allen was later awarded the Medal of Honor.

Files of the National Archives. Adapted from www.magweb.com, "ACW Heroics" by Russ Lockwood. Used by written permission.

**

On the eastern slopes of South Mountain, it was becoming harder to see, between the shadows of the late afternoon and the dense canopy of gunsmoke hanging over the trees. As the Seventy-sixth New York exchanged fire with a line of Confederates some 100 feet in front of them in an open field, Pvt. Uberto Burnham thought he saw a Rebel officer mounted on horseback giving orders to his men. He said to the boy who stood just in front of him, "Charley Roundy, stand aside." The lad quickly gave way, and Burnham, a skilled marksman, carefully aimed and slowly squeezed the trigger. Much to his surprise, he saw nothing fall, but he was convinced that he had squarely hit his target. Just then, the regiment was flanked and hit with a volley that killed its color bearer, Sgt. Charles Stamp.

The next morning, well after the Confederates had departed South Mountain, Burnham went exploring, hoping to find evidence that he had indeed killed the Rebel leader. Instead of a dead man, Burnham saw only a large tree stump with a large sliver reaching far above it. Through the hazy smoke and confusion of battle, he had mistaken its unusual form for a Confederate officer on horseback. His aim had been fine; his identification of the target faulty. Fifty-eight years later, Burnham returned to South Mountain for a veterans' reunion and looked in vain for the stump he had shot during the battle, but it had long since been removed from the field.

Uberto A. Burnham, "South Mountain – Maryland Campaign," *The National Tribune*, 1928.

**

On the Confederate side, visibility wasn't much better. The Seventh Virginia was in an open stand of timber, sheltered behind large boulders and fallen timbers, with their enemy occupying a skirt of woods opposite a strip of cleared land. For two hours, the two sides blazed away, with neither side able to advance through the killing zone in between the opposing lines. Several Union attempts failed, and it was not until darkness fell that they renewed the attack. To one flank was a cornfield, now completely cut down by the musketry and tramping of soldiers. Suddenly the cry came among the Confederate ranks, "There they are, men! Fire on them!" The stillness of the night was interrupted by sheets of flame accompanied by a deafening crash from the guns of the combatants, plainly disclosing them to be within a few feet of each other. So close were they that Pvt. David Johnston believed that the flame from the respective opposing muskets seemed to intermingle. The well-directed fire of the Confederates caused confusion in the Union ranks and finally compelled them to retire.

By 9:00 p.m., the firing had finally died out on much of South Mountain, which was now shrouded in total darkness. The night air was rent with the shrieks and moans of the wounded and dying soldiers, and doctors and stewards dashed among the mangled bodies looking for those who could be aided. Johnston's Company D of the Seventh Virginia had carried forty men into the fighting at Second Manassas, losing sixteen. After crossing the Potomac and arriving at South Mountain, they had twenty-one officers and men remaining in the ranks. The fight on the slopes near Turner's Gap had cost them four more. By Antietam, they were at half strength compared with a month before. Their story was similar to much of Lee's army.

David E. Johnston, *The Story of a Confederate Boy in the Civil War.* (Portland, Oregon: Glass & Prudhomme Company, 1914).

Monday, September 15, 1862

At early dawn, tens of thousands of foot-weary soldiers were converging on Sharpsburg from opposite directions. Among them was James Kemper's brigade, including the Seventeenth Virginia of Col. Montgomery Corse. The colonel sent ahead foragers to secure food and fresh water for the tired troops. Pvt. Alexander Hunter and two comrades grabbed their respective companies' canteens, left the dusty roadside campsite, and picked their way across the fields to a well-kept brick residence about three miles from Sharpsburg. Getting no response to repeated knocks on the front door, they cautiously entered the tidy abode. The owners had recently left, and now the only inhabitant was the family's pet cat, happily sunning itself on a window sill.

Finding that the cupboard, "like that of an ancient miser," and the kitchen were bare, Hunter and his friends left the home and filled their canteens with ice cold water from a nearby spring. Noticing a small dairy at the foot of the hill, they made their way there and, to their astonishment and delight, discovered that someone had left at its door several buckets and cans of fresh milk, over which rich, yellow cream had risen. Pouring out the suddenly uninteresting spring water, the Rebels soon filled their old canteens with milk.

One of the Virginians noticed that the dairy had a loft, so the trio climbed up to investigate what it might contain. It turned out to be a storeroom, filled with several barrels sitting on wooden stands. The curious Rebels cracked open one of the barrels, and discovered them to contain apple cider. Out went the cold milk; into the canteens went the cider. Soon, an exclamation of joy from one of the party drew the other two to his side by another barrel, which turned out to be filled with apple brandy. Of course, out went the cider and in gurgled the golden alcohol.

The squad debated what to do. Some wanted to roll the heavy barrel of brandy back to camp and ignore everything else in the loft. However, the sergeant, wishing to obey the colonel's strict orders to take only food, refused to allow it. The debate grew heated, and the sergeant decided to end matters once and for all. He crashed in the barrel head with the butt of his musket, and "the precious stream, which would have made glad, for a time at least, the whole brigade, poured in a useless stream upon the floor."

The dismayed soldiers sullenly snatched up a half dozen tubs of apple butter from the storeroom and headed back outside. Seeing flashes of burnished steel off in the distance, they raced ahead to catch up with their brigade on its march to destiny at Antietam. Breathlessly, they distributed the canteens to their respective owners, who gulped down the precious brandy. Colonel Corse blessed Hunter and the foragers as he took "a long, lover-like kiss from the mouth of my canteen." Hunter had intended to save a little of the brandy in case he was wounded in the upcoming fight, but to his dismay, Corse had polished off the last drop.

Alexander Hunter, *Johnny Reb and Billy Yank*. (New York and Washington: The Neale Publishing Company, 1905).

**

In the days that followed the fight for South Mountain, dozens of Confederate stragglers and deserters were rounded up. As the heavily depleted Seventy-sixth New York Infantry prepared to move westward through the Pleasant Valley towards Sharpsburg, Private Van Valkenburg was on duty at headquarters. Before the regiment moved out, he started out to explore the neighborhood, most likely seeking something for the headquarters' mess. Riding to a nearby farmhouse, he saw seven Confederate soldiers seated near the house with their rifles stacked a few yards away from them. Drawing his pistol, he calmly approached the septet and ordered them to fall in. One of the Confederates started to reach for his rifle, but Van Valkenburg, with his pistol pointed directly at the Rebel, gave him a stern warning and he fell in with the rest.

They were directed to march towards the regiment's headquarters, but on the way they came across two other Confederates, who were ordered into line with the seven. Van Valkenburg, riding behind the prisoners, escorted them all into Federal lines. For his deed, he was offered a commission as a lieutenant. However, he declined the promotion, saying he had no education and that he could fill best the position he now had.

Uberto A. Burnham, "South Mountain – Maryland Campaign," *The National Tribune*, 1928.

**

Sightseeing and souvenir hunting often followed the cessation of combat. As he walked around the slopes near Turner's Gap during the morning, Capt. Henry F. Noyes' attention was drawn to the dead body of a young Rebel lieutenant, whose serene appearance portrayed a "very handsome face and placid expression." He stood and looked down earnestly at the corpse, trying to read in the pale countenance some fragments of the dead officer's life history. Noyes wondered if perhaps the plain gold ring on his finger might give him the key to his whole life-story. He walked away to the left for more exploring, but soon returned. The ground around Noyes was strewn with muskets, swords, and military trappings of every description. Some Federal soldiers were busy picking up these spoils of war, and Noyes noted two or three kneeling and stooping around the fallen Confederate lieutenant. Hastening his pace, he was "horrified to witness one wretch trying to force off with his knife the plain gold ring. I have rarely been more indignant, and drove the harpy off from his prey."

George F. Noyes, *The Bivouac and the Battle-Field; or, Campaign Sketches in Virginia and Maryland* (New York: Harper & Brothers, 1863)

**

Typically after most Civil War battles, many local civilians roamed the battlefield to gawk at the scenes of destruction and to pocket a few souvenirs, despite the entreaties of the provost guard. South Mountain was no different. Dr. Thomas Ellis, the surgeon of the Twelfth New York, watched with amusement as area farmers pored over the fields and woods to collect portable relics, including cartridge boxes, bayonet scabbards, old muskets, and even unexploded artillery shells.

Thomas T. Ellis, *Leaves from the Diary of an Army Surgeon; or, Incidents of Field, Camp, and Hospital Life.* (New York: John Bradburn, 1863).

**

In other cases, the discoveries were far grimmer than mere souvenirs. Young Frank Firey and his father were among those civilians searching the fields near Fox's Gap. They encountered the corpse of a fair-haired Georgia lad, who appeared to be about 18 years old. Rifling through his pocket, they found a letter from his sister, who had poignantly wrote, "Hurry up and whip the Yankees and come home." Shot through the forehead by one of those Yankees, he never would return home to his anxious family.

Frank P. Firey, "On the Battle Field of South Mountain," *Confederate Veteran*, Volume XXIII, 1919.

**

As the Sixth New Hampshire marched across Fox's Gap high on South Mountain the morning after the battle, they encountered a large number of dead Rebels. Not far away, one lone Confederate soldier was sitting astride a stone "rail-and-rider" wall. Sgt. William W. French of Company B decided to approach the solitary figure and see what he wanted, as it was curious that the Reb was so calm while the Yankees passed by. Going near, French asked him what he wanted. French's superior, Lt. Thomas J. Carleton, called to him and asked him what the "Johnnie" had said. Soon, French was close enough to see, to his amazement, that the serene Southerner was in actuality quite dead. He had apparently been shot while crossing the stone wall, and one of the wooden stakes now held him fixed in an upright position.

Capt. Lyman Jackman, *History of the Sixth New Hampshire Regiment in the War for the Union.* (Concord, New Hampshire: Republican Press Association, 1891).

39

**

Not everyone discovered by the advancing Yankees was dead. One soldier in the Seventy-sixth New York was exploring when he encountered a young Rebel playing possum. The startled Southerner drawled, "Don't shoot! Don't shoot! I am your prisoner." The Federal corralled him and escorted him back to Brig. Gen. John Hatch's provost. Apparently as if to justify why he was still alive in a field teeming with the dead and dying, the shaken boy whined, "I told them I was a coward and couldn't fight, but they drove me up here, where I came near to being killed." He explained, "So I dropped, and crawled behind a stump and waited there all night."

Abram P. Smith, *History of the Seventy-sixth Regiment New York Volunteers*. (Courtland, New York: 1876).

**

As the One Hundred and Twenty-fourth Pennsylvania traversed South Mountain the day after the battle, Pvt. George D. Miller was sickened to see a cartload of amputated limbs, mostly legs that had been cut off above the knee. "It made a great impression on me, as losing a limb was the only thing I dreaded when I decided to enlist." At Antietam, Miller would be seriously wounded in the stomach, but he recovered to fight again, complete with all of his extremities.

Robert M. Green, ed., *History of the One Hundred and Twenty-fourth Regiment Pennsylvania Volunteers*. (Philadelphia: Ware Bros. Company, 1907).

**

As John Gibbon's "Black Hat Brigade" descended South Mountain on the National Road turnpike, they were greeted by a group of gray-haired local citizens who, "almost frantic with joy," came rushing up to greet them. The old men waved their hats, laughed, and cried unashamedly. One particular gent trotted alongside the horse of Maj. Rufus Dawes of the Sixth Wisconsin and exuberantly commented, "We have watched for you, Sir, and we have prayed for you and now thank God you have come." Overcome with emotion, he climbed the bank alongside the road and began to shout, loudly thanking God. As Dawes turned around on his horse to watch the senior citizen, the next regiment in line, the Nineteenth Indiana, began to lustily cheer the man.

Rufus R. Dawes, *Service with the Sixth Wisconsin Volunteers*. (Marietta, Ohio: E. R. Alderman, 1890).

**

D. H. Hill's stubborn defense of South Mountain had bought enough time for Stonewall Jackson to invest Harper's Ferry and force most of its 12,000-man garrison to surrender on September 15 – the largest mass surrender of United States Army forces

40

until Corregidor during World War II. Surrounded on three sides with Confederate artillery now on the heights that dominated the river town, Col. Dixon Miles believed that further resistance was useless, although several of his officers disagreed. He reluctantly pulled down Old Glory from its pole about nine a.m. and ran up the white flag. Not long afterwards, he was mortally wounded by a shell fragment.

However, his garrison's U.S. flag was safe. It seems that a plucky Irish woman, "of Amazonian size, and heart as loyal and brave," had taken possession of it, and several months later met with Maj. Gen. Robert C. Schenck, who by then commanded the Middle Military Department from his headquarters in Baltimore. Schenck escorted her to Washington, D.C., where together they met with Secretary of War Edwin M. Stanton to formally present Miles' flag to the War Department. An incredulous Stanton inquired, "How did you secure this, my excellent woman?" She proudly replied, "Sure, sir, I just lifted my clothes, and wrapped it round me here, just as they [Jackson's Rebels] flocked into the parade." Stanton thanked her for her devotion and ordered that she be rewarded with $50.

Richard M. Devens, *The Pictorial Book of Anecdotes and Incidents of the War of the Rebellion, Civil, Military, Naval and Domestic...* (Hartford, Connecticut: Hartford Publishing Co., 1866).

**

Instead of surrendering, well over a thousand Union cavalrymen had slipped away during the previous night, riding undetected through a gap in the Rebel lines towards Sharpsburg and safety. In other cases, individual soldiers also chose not to surrender. During the afternoon, the Third Pennsylvania Cavalry of the Army of the Potomac was on patrol not far from Harper's Ferry. As they descended a mountain slope, the advance guard was startled by two distant men who suddenly jumped down from the trees. Galloping up to investigate, they were surprised to find that the mysterious duo were fellow Union soldiers, infantrymen from a Maryland regiment who had escaped Harper's Ferry by swimming across the swift river and hiding. The pair shocked the Pennsylvanians by reporting that Harper's Ferry had surrendered. They were soon ushered up the command chain to General McClellan, who then learned of the disaster that had befallen Colonel Miles' large garrison.

Regimental History Committee, *History of the Third Pennsylvania Cavalry, Sixtieth Regiment Pennsylvania Volunteers in the American Civil War 1861-1865.* (Philadelphia: Franklin Printing Company, 1905).

**

For thousands of years, the public has been fascinated by glimpses of famous celebrities, whether they were political leaders, military officers, or civilians in the limelight. The Civil War soldier was not immune to this desire to personally see those of notoriety. Hundreds of Union prisoners of war were lounging around Harper's Ferry awaiting disposition when Stonewall Jackson arrived in the vicinity. According to one

South Carolinian who was guarding them, "The Federals were never weary of extolling his genius and inquiring for particulars of his history. They were extremely anxious to see him. He came up from the riverside late in the afternoon. The intelligence spread like electricity. Almost the whole mass of prisoners broke over us, rushed to the road, threw up their hats, cheered, roared, bellowed as even Jackson's own troops had scarcely ever done. We, of course, joined in with them. The general gave a stiff acknowledgement of the compliment, pulled down his hat, drove his spurs into his horse and went clattering down the hill away from the noise." For these Yankees, hero worship extended even to the enemy. One man had an echo of response all about him when he said aloud: "Boys, he's not much for looks, but if we'd had him we wouldn't have been caught in this trap!"

Yates Snowden, ed., *History of South Carolina* Volume II (Chicago and New York: Lewis Printing, 1920)
Henry K. Douglas, "Stonewall Jackson in Maryland," *Battles and Leaders of the Civil War*, Volume II. (New York: The Century Co., 1887-88).

**

Prior to the surrender, many of the Federal soldiers had been outfitted with fresh new uniforms and accoutrements from the burgeoning Harper's Ferry supply depot. As a long column of Rebels passed along one of the streets, the crowd of freshly clad Yankee prisoners and the rag-tag veterans of the Army of Northern Virginia needled one another. One "blue-belly" called out, "Hello, Johnny, why don't you wear better clothes?" In an instant, an old North Carolinian retorted, "These are good enough to kill hogs in."

George Baylor, *Bull Run to Bull Run, or Four Years in the Army of Northern Virginia.* (Richmond: B. F. Johnson Publishing Company, 1900).

**

Before the Confederates began entering Sharpsburg in force in midday, most of its 2,000 residents fled into the countryside, taking with them as many valuables as they could carry and leading their livestock and horses to safety. Some buried their treasures in their yards; others secreted them in hiding places in houses and outbuildings. The majority of the townspeople who left were pro-Union or neutral in their politics. Some secessionist supporters had remained behind, and, as Lee's troops filed into town, they began to point out the empty houses of the prominent Union men, hoping that the Rebels would deal with them accordingly. Over the next couple of days, the Confederates obliged. According to war correspondent and artist Alfred Waud, who surveyed the scene after the battle, "All that was eatable was eaten up, blankets they stole, and furniture they destroyed, even digging up things that the inhabitants had cached." Disgusted at the behavior of the pro-Southern Sharpsburg citizens, he added, "It would be a good idea to confiscate their goods for the benefit of the sufferers."

Harper's Weekly, October 11, 1862.

**

The Thirty-fifth Massachusetts, a green regiment that had just experienced its first combat the day before, started down the western slope of South Mountain about two o'clock in the afternoon. They had an inauspicious beginning when Pvt. Greenleaf F. Jellison of Company C accidentally shot himself in his foot shortly after the regiment started its march. Not long afterwards, the men spotted two young bulls, one black and one reddish in color, in a field alongside the road. Taking advantage of broken fences, the two bulls were having a pitched battle of their own. The boys soon nicknamed one bull "Mac" and the other "Bob Lee," and quickly chose favorites as they watch the beasts struggle. After some debate, they declared Mac the winner of the contest.

The History of the Thirty-Fifth Massachusetts Volunteer Infantry Regiment, 1862-1865, with a Roster. (Boston: Regimental Association, 1884).

**

As the soldiers of the Thirty-ninth Massachusetts marched towards Sharpsburg, they had to endure a twenty-five mile march on dusty roads in broiling sunshine. They appropriated a large goose along the way, intending to cook the weighty fowl for their dinner. Their strength and stamina drooped as the day wore on, and the goose seemed heavier and heavier each hour. One by one, the struggling soldiers passed the dead bird from man to man. Finally, they grew tired of carrying the goose and left its body by the road for some luckier party that might come along later in the long column. The Bay Staters must have been totally exhausted to leave behind such a tasty edible.

Alfred S. Roe, *The Thirty-ninth Regiment Massachusetts Volunteers 1862-1865.* (Worchester, Massachusetts: Regimental Veteran Association, 1914).

Chapter 3
Antietam

Tuesday, September 16, 1862

Morning dawned hot and "intensely sultry," with a heavy and dense fog that hampered and, at times, suspended the movement of troops and batteries. By eleven o'clock, a slight breeze had risen, which soon dissipated much of the haze. The sky became slightly overcast with thin clouds, making the heat more tolerable for the thousands of soldiers toiling in the Sharpsburg area. Durell's Battery of Pennsylvania light artillery was among the many Union batteries to unlimber and establish sight lines. They were in a little triangular patch of woods facing the distant scenic Antietam Creek and a small stone bridge that within twenty-four hours would gain immortality as "Burnside's Bridge." For now, all was peaceful on their front, although a prolonged artillery duel soon raged to their right.

Pennsylvania at Antietam (Harrisburg: Harrisburg Publishing Company, 1907).

**

Early in the morning, a small scouting party from the Fifteenth Pennsylvania Cavalry, under Maj. Frank Ward, encountered a woman on the road outside of Hagerstown. She informed the Yankee horsemen that a party of Rebels was at her sister's house getting breakfast. As the house was nearby, Ward dispatched youthful Sgt. Harry C. Butcher with two troopers to capture them. Butcher and his comrades galloped to the house, stopped outside the door, jumped off their horses, and swiftly entered the house. Brandishing cocked Navy pistols, the trio surprised the Confederates, who quickly surrendered without a fight. When they finally had a chance to assess the situation, the five Rebs, all adult men, were supremely chagrined to learn that their captors were inexperienced boys from a newly raised regiment, one that had been in Federal service a mere three weeks.

Fred J. Anspach, "At Antietam," *History of the Fifteenth Pennsylvania Volunteer Cavalry...* (Charles H. Kirk, editor) (Philadelphia: Historical Committee of the Society of the Fifteenth Pennsylvania Cavalry, 1906).

**

The Rebels were not the only ones taking possessions and provisions from the Marylanders. The quartermaster of the One Hundred and Twenty-fourth Pennsylvania somehow procured a herd of steers and drove them into the regiment's campsite during the early evening, where they were slaughtered and cooked. Cpl. David Wilkinson and his comrades feasted heartily, as all they had eaten all day on the hard march towards Sharpsburg were a few army crackers. For Wilkinson, the roasted beef would be his last meal with his regiment, as he would be critically wounded the following day and discharged from the service in November to convalesce at home.

Robert M. Green, ed., *History of the One Hundred and Twenty-fourth Regiment Pennsylvania Volunteers.* (Philadelphia: Ware Bros. Company, 1907).

**

The Seventeenth Virginia's opening shots at Antietam satisfied a personal need more pressing than killing Yankees. Stationed in a ravine some 500 yards from Cemetery Hill on the outskirts of Sharpsburg, the men were becoming callous and indifferent towards the upcoming fight, as their bellies were empty (the six tubs of apple butter purloined from the dairy the day before now being gone). Less than fifty men now remained from the eight hundred or so that had fought in the regiment's first battle, and, by now, no one shrunk from combat, but the lack of food had become a problem that needed immediate resolution. It seems that a "foolish, innocent, confiding cow – with a pathetic look in her big eyes and all unknowing of soldiers' ways," had grazed her way near the regiment's line. A dozen bullets went crashing into her skull before she knew what hit her. A score of knives flashed in the sunlight as ravenous Rebels soon turned the bovine into beefsteak. "Everything was soon eaten, even the tail, which but a short hour ago had been calmly and quietly switching flies from her back."

Alexander Hunter, *Johnny Reb and Billy Yank.* (New York and Washington: The Neale Publishing Company, 1905).

**

Throughout the long day, soldiers on both sides passed the time while awaiting orders. Prolonged artillery duels were never popular, as often soldiers would lie prone for hours to avoid being targeted. Maj. Charles Chipman of the Twenty-ninth Massachusetts echoed the feelings of many soldiers that day. "I dislike this shelling very much. It is harmless compared to infantry fighting, …[which] is very exciting and a person thinks but little of it while they are engaged. While under artillery fire alone the Infantry are lying down and can do nothing." The next day, he got his wish as the regiment, the only non-Irish unit in the famed Irish Brigade, saw plenty of infantry fighting.

Charles Chipman papers, U.S. Army Military History Institute, Carlisle, Pennsylvania

**

According to one local woman, Mary Bedinger Mitchell, the remaining residents of Sharpsburg reacted quickly to the sudden onset of angry artillery shells. "The better people kept some outward coolness, with perhaps a feeling of 'noblesse oblige' – but the poorer classes acted as if the town were already in a blaze, and rushed from their houses with their families and household goods to make their way into the country. The road was thronged, the streets blocked; men were vociferating, women crying, children screaming; wagons, ambulances, guns, caissons' horsemen, footmen, all mingled – and jammed together –in one struggling, shouting mass. The negroes were the worst, and with faces of a ghastly ash-color, and staring eyes, they swarmed into the fields, carrying their babies, their clothes, their pots and kettles, fleeing from the wrath behind them…They fled widely and camped out of range, nor would they venture back for days." War had come to the once obscure town, and it would never again be the same.

Mary Bedinger Mitchell, "A Woman's Recollection of Antietam," *Battles and Leaders of the Civil War*, Volume II. (New York: The Century Co., 1887-88).

**

The cacophony of an angry and prolonged exchange of artillery fire reverberated across the southern Maryland hills late on the day. The venerable Maj. Gen. Edwin V. Sumner, commander of the Union II Corps, casually lay on the grass under a shade tree in front of the brick Pry house, which served as the headquarters for the Army of the Potomac. In an open field a few yards from the reposing general, a party of staff officers and some civilian observers was suddenly startled by a stray Confederate shell, which dropped about a hundred yards from them. Soon, a second shell struck even closer to the group, and the men scattered in all directions with great alacrity. "Why," casually remarked Sumner with a peculiar smile, "those shells excite a good deal of commotion from those young gentlemen!" Nicknamed "Bull" during his lengthy military career, the combat-experienced Sumner was greatly amused that anyone would be disconcerted merely by a few errant shells.

Frank Moore, *Anecdotes, Poetry, and Incidents of the War: North and South. 1860-1865.* (New York: Publication office, Bible house, J. Porteus, agent, 1867).

**

A number of civilians had accompanied the Army of the Potomac to Sharpsburg; some with newspaper credentials, but the majority were simply people interested in seeing some potential combat action. A. D. Richardson and a friend had spent the early part of September 16 loitering around the headquarters of Maj. Gen. Joseph Hooker of the I Corps. Too close to the action for their comfort, bullets knocked a number of Hooker's staff from their horses and shells plowed the ground under their own horses, kicking up a cloud of dust. Hooker soon leaped his white charger over a low fence and galloped thirty yards to the safety of an orchard, with his remaining staff and the pair of terrorized civilians in tow.

There, they had overheard Hooker's thrice-repeated desperate plea for a particular artillery captain to bring up his battery to play on the distant Confederate lines near the East Woods. Once the requested battery was finally in action, the Rebels wavered and Hooker ordered in the infantry. He and his aides rode forward to press the attack. Richardson, by now "having shared the experience of 'Fighting Joe Hooker' long enough," turned and headed to the rear. He noted the arrival of fresh reinforcements, as well as a substantial number of stragglers, who were arrayed in "long lines behind rocks and trees." Like the civilian duo, these soldiers preferred the relative safety of the rear.

As he later leisurely rode down a grassy slope in the darkness, his reverie was broken by more Rebel artillery fire. One solid shot whizzed by, fanning his face with a rush of air and causing his horse to rear almost upright. Another projectile soon whistled by, and, by the light of a huge bonfire of farmer's rail fences, he noted that it bounded "like a foot-ball" into a long column of infantry, who ignored their fallen comrades and immediately closed up ranks.

By 9 p.m., Richardson and his friend Smalley had arrived at a farmhouse where Union pickets offered some protection. They dared not light candles or a fire, as it was within range of Confederate sharpshooters. He tied his horse to an apple tree and lay down on the parlor floor, using his saddle as a pillow. He spent a restless night listening to the pop-pop of occasional skirmishing. At dawn, the picket officer shook his arm, woke Richardson, and advised him to immediately leave, as "this place is getting rather hot for civilians." Having seen enough of the front lines, Richardson rode his horse to the extreme rear, where he spent September 17 watching the battle from a ridge near McClellan's headquarters.

Frank Moore, *Anecdotes, Poetry, and Incidents of the War: North and South. 1860-1865.* (New York: Publication office, Bible house, J. Porteus, agent, 1867).

**

Early in the evening, contact was made between elements of Hooker's I Corps and Confederates under John Bell Hood. As the First Texas of Hood's Division was going into line, Pvt. Thomas Jefferson Bowman slipped away from Company M and hid in the upper story of a building about 150 yards from where the Yankees were crossing the creek. Peering out a window, he could see them distinctly and could not resist the temptation to shoot. Bowman fired about sixty shots at the Federals before they located him and finally dislodged him. They trained a piece of artillery on the house, and, when the first shot passed completely through it, Jeff 'skeddadled' back to his regiment. Hooker deployed George Meade's Pennsylvania Reserve Division for the attack on Hood's line in the East Woods. The initial infantry action at Antietam was about to begin.

Adapted from Scott Hosier, "Savage Skirmish near Sharpsburg," *America's Civil War,* September 1998, quoting an eyewitness account.

**

As the Thirteenth Pennsylvania "Bucktails" advanced through a plowed field towards the East Woods and Hood's waiting Rebels, they were exposed to a murderous storm of lead. Dropping flat on their faces, they returned fire with their breech-loading rifles. Every now and then, they would rise and dash forward a few yards before going prone again. Only a few feet away from the fence line that marked the edge of the woods, Col. McNeil sprang to his feet and cried, "Forward, Bucktails, forward!" Those were his last words, as he was quickly cut down and pitched lifeless to the dirt. His men, mad with fury, leaped up and cleared the fence, driving off the defenders. McNeil still had the lucky bullet from South Mountain tucked in his pocket.

O. R. Howard Thompson and William H. Rauch, *History of the Bucktails, Kane Rifle Regiment of the Pennsylvania Reserve Corps.* (Philadelphia: Electric Printing Company, 1906).

**

Capt. James Garnett and his comrades in the famed "Stonewall Brigade" were exhausted after weeks of seemingly endless marching and fighting. Earlier in the day, they had been moved to an open field on the left of Jackson's defensive line, with their right flank anchored on the Hagerstown Pike north of Sharpsburg. They were subjected to a galling crossfire from the Union batteries to their front and from McClellan's heavy guns beyond Antietam Creek on their right rear. The shelling continued late into the night, but it "did not do much damage and served only as a fine display of pyrotechnics." Despite the roar of the guns and the vivid flashes from the exploding shells overhead, the weary Virginia troops were soon unconscious in profound slumber. Col. Andrew J. Grigsby and his staff, including Captain Garnett, secured a comfortable fence panel and were soon imitating the men around them, sound asleep and oblivious to the shelling. For many of the venerated Stonewall Brigade, this would be their last night on earth.

James M. Garnett and Alexander Hunter, "The Battle of Antietam or Sharpsburg," *Southern Historical Society Papers*, Vol. XXXI. (Richmond: Virginia, 1903).

**

Nearly everyone knew the morrow would bring a major battle, the second one in less than a month for many of the men. Men contemplated their futures, wrote letters home, prayed or read their Testaments, cleaned their weapons, or quietly conversed with comrades. After particularly inquiring if his adjutant had fully completed the muster rolls for the regiment, Col. Richard Oakford of the One Hundred and Thirty-second Pennsylvania smiled ruefully and quietly remarked, "We shall not all be here tomorrow night." His prediction was correct, unfortunately. Oakford would be killed the next day, along with thousands of other soldiers.

Frederick L. Hitchcock, *War From the Inside: The Story of the 132nd Regiment Pennsylvania Volunteer Infantry in the War for the Suppression of the Rebellion.* (Philadelphia: J. B. Lippincott, 1904).

**

Long after firing ceased, General Hood was concerned that the commotion he was hearing over in the Union lines meant that they were massing fresh troops to renew the fight in the morning. Seeking reinforcements and wanting to send his men to the rear to get much-needed food, he rode off in the darkness to search for his commander, Stonewall Jackson. He found him, alone and soundly sleeping by the root of a tree. Jackson arose, ordered three brigades to replace Hood's division in the line, and approved his request to pull back. A grateful Hood quickly rode off in search of his wagons, so that the men could prepare and cook their flour (the only food they had). Unfortunately, the wagons were so far in the rear and the night was so dark that Hood did not get them in position until nearly dawn. As the famished men began preparing the dough, an officer of Alexander Lawton's staff dashed up to Hood, exclaiming, "General Lawton sends his compliments with the request that you come at once to his support." The call to arms was instantly sounded and Hood's soldiers again marched to the front, leaving their uncooked rations in camp. The bloodiest day in American military history was underway.

John Bell Hood, *Advance and Retreat: Personal Experiences in the United States and Confederate States Armies*. (Burk & McFetridge, 1880).

Wednesday, September 17, 1862

Fighting began in earnest very early on the morning of Wednesday, September 17, when General McClellan launched a series of relatively uncoordinated attacks aimed at pushing through Confederate lines north of Sharpsburg. A hot, dry southwestern wind pushed aside the fog bank that shrouded the top of nearby South Mountain, which still teemed with the dead and wounded. However, in the verdant fields around Antietam Creek, billowing clouds of gunsmoke soon hampered visibility as "Fighting Joe" Hooker's I Corps advanced. Bullets and shell fragments whizzed through the dawn air, maiming or killing hundreds of soldiers – officers and enlisted men alike. Maj. Gen. George G. Meade was struck by a spent canister shot, leaving him with a severe contusion on his right thigh, and his famed warhorse "Old Baldy" was shot through the neck by a Minié ball and temporarily disabled. Both horse and rider lived, and Meade would go on to fame as the victorious commander of the Army of the Potomac at Gettysburg. Surviving the war by many years, Old Baldy's stuffed head would later be displayed in a Philadelphia museum.

George Meade Jr., *The Life and Letters of General Meade: Major General United States Army*. (New York: Charles Scribner's Sons, 1913).

**

General Lee, normally stoic and calm as battle loomed, allowed his emotions to betray him. As he was riding in the rear lines, he encountered a soldier surreptitiously toting a freshly killed pig. Enraged, Lee ordered the thief to be arrested. As an example to discourage other pilferers, he was to be escorted to Stonewall Jackson and shot for his wanton disobedience of Lee's strict orders against foraging. Short of men already, Jackson soon commuted the execution sentence, and instead ordered the man to be sent straight to the front lines. He was to be placed in a position where the odds were highest he would be shot by the Yankees. The culprit fought well, survived the battle, and redeemed himself through his bravery under the scathing fire. He later became regarded as the man who had lost the pig, but "saved his bacon."

Armistead L. Long, *Memoirs of Robert E. Lee: His Military and Personal History.* (London: Sampson Low, Marston, Searle, and Rivington, 1886).

**

Reporter Charles Coffin of the Boston *Journal* had accompanied the Union army as a war correspondent. Dressed in civilian clothes and wearing an old dilapidated hat, Coffin had left Hagerstown early in the morning, hoping to reach Sharpsburg via the turnpike and see the battle from the Confederate perspective, a "grand accomplishment if successful," much like "going behind the scenes of a theater." A refugee had informed him that the tollgate two miles north of Sharpsburg was held by Rebels, and that became Coffin's objective.

Approaching Sharpsburg, the solitary horseman encountered a group of concerned farmers, who were "listening with dazed countenances to the uproar momentarily increasing in volume. It was no longer alone the boom of the batteries, but a rattle of musketry – at first like pattering drops upon a roof; then a roll, crash, roar, and rush, like a mighty ocean billow upon the shore, chafing the pebbles, wave on wave, – with deep and heavy explosions of the batteries, like the crashing of thunderbolts. I think the currents of air must have had something to do with the effect of sound. The farmers were walking about nervously, undecided, evidently, whether to flee or to remain."

As Coffin slowed to greet the farmers, one of them called out, "I wouldn't go down the pike if I were you. You will ride right into the Rebs." The intrepid reporter replied, "That is just where I would like to go." The response from another farmer jolted Coffin into sensibility, "You can't pass yourself off for a Reb; they'll see, the instant they set eyes on you, that you are a Yank. They'll gobble you up and take you to Richmond."

Indeed, Coffin apparently looked far more Yankee than Rebel. As he later wrote, "No doubt I acted wisely in leaving the turnpike and riding to gain the right flank of the Union line. A short distance and I came upon a Confederate soldier lying beneath a tree. He doubtless supposed that I was a cavalryman, and raised his hand as if to implore me not to shoot him. His face was pale and haggard, and the lad dropped from the ranks through sheer exhaustion. I left the poor fellow with the conviction that he never again would see his Southern home."

Charles C. Coffin, "Antietam Scenes," *Battles and Leaders of the Civil War*, Volume II. (New York: The Century Co., 1887-88).

**

For part of the early battle, Stonewall Jackson established his headquarters at the Dunker Church, a simple whitewashed wood-frame structure erected in 1852 as the meeting house of the local German Reformed Brethren congregation. Jackson, whose men were heavily engaged at the time, asked a courier to take a message to Maj. Gen. D. H. Hill. Before the soldier left, he drew his canteen and offered Jackson a swig of fresh milk. During the early morning, before he went into combat, the man had taken the time to milk a cow in a meadow behind the woods adjacent to the small church.

Files of the Antietam National Battlefield, National Park Service.

**

As the battle intensified, the unarmed noncombatants faced several choices – seek safety in the rear, stay and minister to the wounded, or shoulder a weapon. Assistant Surgeon J.C. Farley of the First Georgia, unable to stand the early morning crash of artillery, broke and looked for shelter, running around senselessly while men of the regiment repeatedly mocked him with cries of "Here is a safe place!" He finally dashed into a small stream that fed Sharpsburg's reservoir. His laughing comrades soon turned back to their grim business.

William H. Andrews, "Tige Anderson's Brigade at Sharpsburg," *Confederate Veteran,* Vo. XVI.

**

By contrast, the gray-haired chaplain of the Twelfth Massachusetts, Israel Washburn, decided to minister to his flock in a different way. He picked up a fallen musket, joined the advanced skirmishers, and joined his congregants in a chorus of gunfire. Not long afterwards, he was knocked to the ground by a sudden violent impact with his chest. Getting up and examining himself, he was relieved to discover that the bullet had caused no real damage. A distant Rebel had scored a direct hit on Washburn's pocket Bible, which had absorbed what might have been a killing blow.

Benjamin F. Cook, *History of the Twelfth Massachusetts Volunteers (Webster Regiment).* (Boston: Twelfth Webster Regiment Association, 1882).

**

Few times up to that point in American history had artillery been so deadly on a battlefield. Shell, shot, and canister swept aside entire groups of men, sometimes as many as a dozen or more at a time. Counter-battery fire and infantry volleys soon knocked some field guns out of commission. As men were killed or fell wounded and maimed, battery commanders scrambled to keep adequate crews healthy enough to maintain the steady volume of fire. Battery B, Fourth United States Artillery was particularly hard hit as it supported the Iron Brigade during the early morning fighting west of farmer D. R. Miller's cornfield. As many as seventeen artillerists were soon dead or wounded. Young bugler John Cook, a fifteen-year-old lad from Cincinnati, coolly ignored the severe enemy fire and joined the remaining cannoneers, loading canister rounds into a 12 lb. Napoleon gun. The resultant blasts repelled three separate Confederate assaults and

51

helped the Second Wisconsin avoid being overrun. Cook would be the youngest recipient of the twenty Medals of Honor later awarded to Antietam veterans.

Files of the Antietam National Battlefield, National Park Service.

**

Amid the thunder of the artillery and the whistling of Minié balls, grown men and boys alike began to challenge their life expectancy. Some of the fainter hearts broke and ran to the rear. One young soldier in the Eighth Pennsylvania Reserves, seeing most of his comrades wilt in the face of a determined Rebel attack near Miller's cornfield, screamed, "Rally boys, rally! Die like men: don't run like dogs!" Only a handful initially joined him, but the Union line held for a while.

Henry Steele Commager, ed., *The Blue and the Gray.* (Indianapolis, Indiana: The Bobbs-Merrill Co., 1950).

**

Actually, contrary to the shouts of the Pennsylvania boy, the dogs weren't running. As the battle of Antietam grew more intense, the little dog "Charlie" that always accompanied the Troup Artillery into battle was in his glory. One of the admiring artillerymen later wrote, "He ran up and down the line from gun to gun. He would wiggle his little body with joy, while his bark rang out with the roar of battle. He seemed not to know fear, and as the battle grew fiercer so did his joy." The dog was with the battery in some of the Civil War's fiercest engagements, from the Peninsula Campaign through Appomattox Court House, and always exhibited the same wild joy and courage. Two days before Lee surrendered in April 1865, a Federal shell struck a tree near where Charlie was standing and exploded, and, when the smoke cleared away, little Charlie was dead. His mournful human companions dug his grave at the foot of a tree. The pet was one of the very last casualties of the veteran battery.

George B. Atkisson, "Charlie: 'Recruit' to Troup Artillery." (*Confederate Veteran,* Vol. XIX).

**

On the Federal side, the mascot of the Tenth Maine, a dog named "Major," also behaved well under fire, barking fiercely and keeping up a steady growl from the time the regiment went into action until it returned to the rear. He contributed his own unique noises to "the uproar that some consider so essential in battle. He had shown so much genuine pluck, moreover, that the men of [Company] H were bragging of his barking, and of his biting at the sounds of the bullets, asserting besides that he was 'tail up' all day."

Maj. John M. Gould, *History of the First – Tenth – Twenty-ninth Maine Regiment* (Portland: Stephen Berry, 1871).

**

As the Iron Brigade advanced along the Hagerstown Turnpike towards the Confederates, they received a galling fire as the Confederates counterattacked from the West Woods. Capt. Werner Von Bachelle, a former officer in the French Army who was schooled in Napoleonic tactics and the doctrine of fatalism, was mortally wounded. Von Bachelle had a pet Newfoundland dog, which he had taught in camp to perform remarkable tricks, as well as certain military salutes. The dog was by his side when the officer fell with several wounds. Later, as the regiment retreated, the men of Company F noted the dog faithfully guarding the body of its master, who had lain down in the turnpike to die. Two days later, when it was finally safe to explore that portion of the battlefield, the Wisconsin boys discovered the animal lying dead across Von Bachelle's corpse. They were buried side by side in a grave near the Miller barn.

Rufus R. Dawes, *Service with the Sixth Wisconsin Volunteers*. (Marietta, Ohio: E. R. Alderman, 1890).

**

Von Bachelle's faithful pet was not the only Newfoundland to perish on America's bloodiest day. Another one served as the unofficial attaché of the Twentieth New York State Militia. The stray had accompanied the regiment since it left Frederick. At South Mountain, the dog had advanced with the regiment, seemingly indifferent to the whistling of the enemy's bullets around him, and to the rattle of the New Yorkers' muskets. Now, at Antietam as the soldiers advanced west of the Hagerstown Pike, he was an "unconcerned spectator," oblivious to the danger. Lt. Col. Theodore Gates later saw him lying on the field on the left of the regiment, near W. H. Pollock of Company H. Both man and beast were dead.

Theodore B. Gates, *The "Ulster Guard" (20th New York State Militia) and the War of the Rebellion*. (New York: Benjamin H. Tyrrel, 1879).

**

Company B of the Fourth Texas kept a white fox terrier as a pet. Nicknamed "Candy" because the dog had been presented to the men by an Austin candy maker shortly after the soldiers enlisted, the pet wore a collar engraved with "Candy, Company B, 4th Texas." The canine had become lost during the Battle of Gaines' Mill earlier in the year, but was located later lying in the arms of the dead soldier who had cared for him. Now, at Antietam, the dog participated in the Texans' attack on Miller's Cornfield. In the swirling fighting, he became separated from his company. A Pennsylvania regiment "captured" Candy, whose whereabouts the rest of the war are still unknown. He was apparently the only dog seized as a prisoner of war at Antietam.

Several other regiments also had dogs with them. "Sallie," the faithful mascot of the Eleventh Pennsylvania, ran out to the regimental skirmish line in Miller's

53

cornfield. She resisted attempts to be sent to the rear, and stayed on the front lines despite being bruised in the side by a spent projectile.

Adapted from Ted Alexander, "Antietam Stories," *Blue & Gray*, Volume XX, Number 1, Fall 2002.

**

Other animals weren't as enthralled as the dogs with the sound and terror of battle. As Capt. James Dinkins and his comrades in the Eighteenth Mississippi advanced though the West Woods towards the distant Yankees, men were falling at every step as shells and shots pounded the earth and cut down the timber. A spotted cow rambled through the line, going to the Mississippians' rear, desperately running like a race horse with her tail high in the air. A Federal artillery shell struck the ground a few feet in front of her and exploded, splattering dirt in all directions and leaving a large hole. The terrified bovine plunged in the hole, but soon scrambled out. Kit Gilmer of Company C hallooed, "Boys, she's a Confederate cow; she's going South!"

James Dinkins, *1861-1865 by an Old Johnnie: Personal Recollections and Experiences in the Confederate Army.* (Cincinnati: The Robert Clarke Company, 1897).

**

One Confederate soldier noted, "During the combat, three pigeons wheeled wildly over the battle field, and raising higher and higher, disappeared in the clouds and ascending smoke. Alas, how many spirits did they accompany on their upward flight from that bloody field of death."

Southern Watchman, October 15, 1862.

**

The pigeons were not the only ones trying to escape the fury of the escalating battle. One civilian, G. Frank Lidy, had been accidentally trapped between the Union and Confederate lines near the Lower (Rohrbach) Bridge, placing him in "a very uncomfortable position," an understatement to say the least. Being a noncombatant, he had nothing with which to defend himself. He embraced the first opportunity to slip away unnoticed to a place of safety. Apparently, Lidy liked the fighting. The following year during the Gettysburg Campaign, he and a party of a dozen friends were captured by Jubal Early's Rebels on South Mountain in southern Pennsylvania while heading for Harrisburg to enlist. Undaunted, Lidy later joined the Twenty-first, and then, in August 1864, the Seventeenth Pennsylvania cavalry regiments.

History of the Seventeenth Regiment Pennsylvania Volunteer Cavalry. (Lebanon, Pennsylvania: Sowers Printing Company, 1911).

**

Artillery boomed across the hillsides, and, in the early morning, the Union I and XII Corps were pounded north of Sharpsburg. To the south, men who were not yet in action took the time to catch up on personal affairs. By eight o'clock, the artillery duel had started to spread to the southern part of the battlefield, and it commenced in earnest an hour later. Soldiers in the Twenty-first Massachusetts of the IX Corps had just received a large quantity of mail about nine o'clock when they were ordered to move out. They were soon repositioned on the reverse slope of a hill near Antietam Creek to support Durell's Battery, which was heavily engaged in counter-battery fire with distant Rebel guns. Capt. Charles Wolcott later wrote, "A good many shot and shell came over us during the following two hours, but we were so well sheltered as to be able to read our home letters, without much danger of getting our heads knocked off."

There was one scary moment for the Bay Staters, however. The regimental color guard was huddled in a tight knot around one of their members who was reading to them from a newspaper that had just arrived. A Rebel shell suddenly descended in their midst and burrowed into the ground at their feet. The resulting explosion threw the colors and men in all directions. Amazingly, one by one, they picked themselves up and discovered that no one had been injured – not even a scratch.

Charles F. Wolcott, *History of the Twenty-first Regiment, Massachusetts Volunteers, in the War for the Preservation of the Union 1861-1865.* (Boston: Houghton, Mifflin and Company, 1882).

**

Amid the crashing of shells and the whizzing of bullets, stewards and soldiers struggled to save the wounded, assisting many to temporary field hospitals in the rear lines. There, in relative safety, surgeons could begin the grim task of treating the victims. Usually, these medical stations were in identifiable landmarks, such as houses, barns, groves, etc. In some cases, they were not far enough from the front lines.

One such hospital was established at the farm of David and Sarah Reel, a middle-aged couple with seven children ranging from five to twenty-seven. The frightened family had left when the armies arrived, and their property served as a staging area for Confederate attacks on the West Woods. Despite being somewhat sheltered by being on the reverse slope of a ridge, their barn lay in the line of fire for long-range Federal artillery. A shell hurtled into the hay-filled barn, exploded, and started a massive fire that soon consumed the structure. Workers were unable to rescue many of the immobile wounded, who died in the conflagration. In the days after the battle, charred human bones were discovered in the ruins by several boys who were exploring the site.

Oliver T. Reilly, *The Battle of Antietam.* (Hagerstown, Maryland: Hagerstown Bookbinding & Printing Co., 1906).

**

Even in the heat of battle, a soldier's thoughts may drift to his stomach. As the Twenty-first New York was traversing a field in between charges, a stray shot struck a

55

large fat pig that had been grunting about in the rear of the regiment, apparently previously indifferent to the sounds of war and the passage of the soldiers. Now the hog squealed in agony. One of the New York boys, seeing an opportunity for a feast after the battle, hastily dropped his musket and ran over to the wounded pig, all the while unsheathing a large knife. With the practiced hand of an experienced butcher, he quickly brought "the lingering sickness of Mr. Pig to an abrupt termination." He rolled the dead animal into a nearby ditch until an opportune time to claim his prize and ran back to his place in the battle line, picked up his musket, and rejoined the fight.

J. Harrison Mills, *Chronicles of the Twenty-first New York State Volunteers…* (Buffalo: 21st Reg't. Veteran Association of Buffalo, 1887)

**

As the Second Pennsylvania Reserves broke under a savage Confederate attack and were driven back across the field, they startled a farmer's chicken, which displayed equal alacrity with the men in its flight to the rear. A very animated race for life or death took place between them. Sergeant-Major Evan Woodward, seizing a favorable opportunity, dove to the ground and captured the prize, which furnished a most sumptuous dinner later that evening after the regiment rallied. Woodward was promoted to adjutant on the battlefield that day.

E. M. Woodward, *Our Campaigns: The Second Regiment Pennsylvania Reserve Volunteers.* (Philadelphia: John E. Potter, 1865).

**

With the early morning repulse of the Union I and XII Corps, General McClellan next sent in the II Corps, which soon became separated in the confusion of combat. John Sedgwick's 5,500-man division advanced east to west and attacked the battered Rebel lines in the West Woods, while two other divisions drifted to the south and eventually attacked additional Confederates lining a sunken farm lane separating the William Roulette and Henry Piper farms.

Often in the confusion and chaos of battle, something familiar can be comforting. The Nineteenth Massachusetts was a part of Sedgwick's Division. After being repulsed in their first attack on the West Woods, they had reformed their battle line and were now again advancing, but the soldiers were wavering in the face of renewed Confederate fire. Col. Edward W. Hinks seized upon an idea to steady his uncertain regiment. He halted it and ordered the men and color guard to form as if on the parade ground. For fifteen minutes, he calmly sat on his horse and drilled the men in the *Manual of Arms* as if they were back in their training camp. He ignored the whistling bullets that occasionally felled one of his men. By the time he ordered "parade rest," the regiment had regained its discipline. Hinks soon renewed the advance with all the coolness and precision of his drill.

Later in the battle as his regiment was in a disadvantaged position, Hinks ordered his men to lie down to avoid murderous fire coming at them from Rebels only

150 yards away. He coolly sat on his horse for half an hour in the incessant storm of lead, "exhibiting no consciousness of danger, but with folded arms, and a smile on his lips…"

R.U. Johnson and C. C. Buel, *Battles and Leaders of the Civil War*, Volume II. (New York: The Century Co., 1887-88).

**

Struck in their left flank about 9:30 a.m. by a savage surprise counterattack, Sedgwick's three brigades quickly melted, suffering some 2,200 casualties in less than twenty minutes. The surviving Federals were sent flying to the rear, seeking shelter wherever they could find it. Among the more fortunate soldiers was George F. Fletcher of the Fifteenth Massachusetts. His Company H was utterly devastated, with only nine of sixty-two men making it back to the rear lines without injury. One of his brothers was killed, but George had somehow remained unhurt in the torrent of projectiles, despite a very close call. Shortly before the battle, the regiment's mail had been delivered, but the men had no time to scan through it. Fletcher had folded a copy of *Harper's Weekly* several times into a compact rectangle and placed it in his blouse pocket, intending to read it later. Jolted by a sudden blow to the chest, he found that he had not been injured. A Confederate Minié ball had struck him in the pocket and pierced the outer layers of the folded newspaper. Its thickness had blunted the impact of the bullet and saved his life. His luck would run out less than a year later, when Fletcher was killed at the Battle of Gettysburg defending against Pickett's Charge.

Andrew E. Ford, *The Story of the Fifteenth Regiment Massachusetts Volunteer Infantry in the Civil War 1861-1864.* (Clinton, Massachusetts: Press of W. J. Coulter, 1898).

**

A couple dozen members of the fleeing Seventy-first Pennsylvania finally reached the Joseph Poffenberger house near the North Woods, where they collapsed from utter exhaustion. Their shattered regiment finally rallied and reformed in a nearby potato patch at the rear of the farmhouse. Hungry and tired, the soldiers whipped out their bayonets and began scratching at the dirt, digging up the potatoes as fast as they could. In the meantime, a few Pennsylvanians entered the abandoned home and discovered, to their delight, several jars of apple butter.

Lt. Benjamin Hibbs noted, "A few unlucky chickens were knocked over, and pot-pies were being prepared with all possible speed." Just as the men of Company D were readying their tasty meal, Confederate artillery began dueling with a nearby Union battery. The shells began dropping into the feasting Federals: "Some [men] were scared badly, some laughed, and some cursed the rebels for the interruption." The shelling compelled the Seventh-first to retire further to the rear to escape the torrent of incoming rounds, and men scrambled to grab the food, utensils, and pots. They carried their treasures several hundred yards to the northeast, where they halted. In a nearby field, they discovered the bodies of several cattle that had recently been dispatched by earlier Rebel shelling. Now safe from further incident, the Pennsylvanians ate a hearty meal and got some much needed rest.

Charles Banes, *History of the Philadelphia Brigade. Sixty-ninth, Seventy-first, Seventy-second, and One hundred and sixth Pennsylvania Volunteers.* (Philadelphia, J.B. Lippincott & Co., 1876).

**

Another survivor of the fierce fighting north of Sharpsburg was a small puppy that belonged to one of the Union batteries (probably Monroe's Battery D, First Rhode Island). In the middle of a booming artillery duel, the little dog, terror-stricken, raced away looking for a safe place to hide. He soon found it, jumping down the shirt of Pvt. Albert Robinson of the One Hundred and Twenty-fifth Pennsylvania.

Regimental Committee, *History of the One Hundred and Twenty-fifth Regiment Pennsylvania Volunteers 1863-1863.* (Philadelphia: J. B. Lippincott, 1906).

**

General Lee skillfully shifted troops around to parry various Federal thrusts, many of which were not coordinated. He ordered Stonewall Jackson to shift some of his artillery from the right flank to the beleaguered lines north of Sharpsburg. As a section of the Rockbridge Artillery galloped by, an artilleryman, black with the grime and powder of a long day's fight, stopped for a moment to salute General Lee, who returned the greeting without recognizing his admirer. It was eighteen-year-old Robert E. Lee, Jr., the general's youngest son, whose countenance and appearance masked his identity. After a brief personal exchange, young Lee raced ahead to rejoin his battery.

Henry K. Douglas, "Stonewall Jackson in Maryland," *Battles and Leaders of the Civil War*, Volume II. (New York: The Century Co., 1887-88).

**

At one point in the smoke-shrouded morning, Stonewall Jackson contemplated a flanking movement around the Federal right to attack them from the rear. However, he was uncertain of the strength and disposition of an enemy force that blocked his path. As the 16-year-old adjutant of the Thirty-fifth North Carolina, Walter Clark, watched from his horse, Pvt. William S. Hood was sent up a tall tree, which he climbed carefully to avoid observation by the enemy. According to Clark, when "Stonewall called out to know how many Yankees he could see over the hill and beyond the East Woods, Hood replied, 'Who-e-e! There are oceans of them, General.' 'Count their flags,' said Jackson sternly, who wished more definite information. This Hood proceeded to do until he had counted thirty-nine, when the General told him that would do and to come down." With so many Yankee regiments in his way, Jackson quickly abandoned the idea of the proposed flank attack.

Walter McK. Clark, *Histories of the Several Regiments and Battalions from North Carolina, in the Great War 1861-'65.* (Raleigh: E.M. Uzzell, 1901).

**

The residents of Sharpsburg huddled in their cellars or ran to find safety as best as they could when the town was subjected to inadvertent artillery fire. According to a newspaper correspondent, "At one house a shell entered the top of the chimney passed down and exploded just above the fire place, knocked out the wall, smashed a sideboard, cut three legs off a table and finally buried itself in the bed. Another passed through the side of a house, missed a pitcher from a table, shivered a looking glass and made its escape through the side of the building and went on its way in search of a rebel. In a two story frame building, the male occupant was looking out of the garret window when a ball struck the house about two feet from the window, glanced to the floor, passed through to the second story, keeled over a chair, dived through the floor, entered a cellar and knocked a washtub into a cocked hat." When the battle was over, a number of Sharpsburg buildings showed the unmistakable scar of war.

Grant County (Wisconsin) Herald, September 24, 1862.

**

As the staff and escort of Brig. Gen. George B. Anderson prepared their meal at a farmhouse used as his brigade headquarters, they were caught in a cross-fire from two Union batteries. Farmer Henry Piper's house, kitchen, surrounding trees, fences, and outbuildings were soon riddled with holes. As Pvt. Walter Battle of the Fourth North Carolina ruefully recalled, "We had a large pot full of chicken on the stove, cooking for dinner, when a bomb took off one-half of the kitchen and turned the stove bottom upwards. That stopped the splendid dinner we had in preparation." General Anderson, denied his piping hot meal, led his brigade in the subsequent fierce fighting at the Sunken Road, where he received a serious wound in his ankle. His wound mortified, and he died on October 16 following surgery to amputate the infected foot.

Laura Elizabeth Lee Battle, *Forget-me-nots of the Civil War; A Romance, Containing Reminiscences and Original Letters of Two Confederate Soldiers.* (St. Louis, Missouri: Press A. R. Fleming Printing Co., c1909).

**

To the average Civil War soldier, the regimental and national flags were objects of reverence. They gave the regiment its identity and provided inspiration and a rallying point during battle. Duty in the color guard during a battle was extremely hazardous, as flag bearers were often deliberately targeted by enemy fire. Still, men risked (and often lost) their lives to defend and protect these colorful pieces of silk. During the heavy fighting just south of Miller's cornfield, three color bearers from the Thirteenth Georgia in Lawton's Brigade were shot down (and brigade commander Col. Marcellus Douglass was killed). The flagstaff had been cut twice by Union fire and now consisted of three distinct pieces. The last of the three color bearers was still alive, although badly wounded. Lying on his back in pain, he nevertheless stubbornly clutched the stump of the shattered flagpole, holding up the Confederate flag until it could be rescued. However, before a comrade could pick up the banner, a shell burst overhead and tore the beautiful folds of the flag into shreds, much to the dismay of the Georgians.

Savannah Republican, October 6, 1862.

**

Among the scores of flag bearers who fell at Antietam was Color Sgt. George Simpson of the One Hundred Twenty-fifth Pennsylvania, shot through the temple. His brother Randolph soon also toppled to the ground, seriously wounded in the chest and incapacitated for the rest of his life. The regiment would lose four more enlisted men who subsequently carried the colors before Capt. William W. Wallace seized the flag, waved it aloft, and finally rallied the broken regiment near a battery. Simpson's carved granite likeness now adorns the regimental monument on Confederate Avenue near the Dunker Church.

Pennsylvania at Antietam (Harrisburg: Harrisburg Publishing Company, 1907)

**

The silken battle flags were not the only sources of colorful inspiration. As the Fifth New Hampshire advanced toward the Piper Farm, Lt. Thomas Livermore was astonished to look at a neighboring regiment and spot the brilliant red shirt of a common private of the Sixty-first New York, who had apparently found a horse and was now riding to and fro along the infantry line when the musketry was hottest. No officer on horseback could be seen, only the courageous enlisted man with his especially conspicuous crimson shirt, who was doing his best to encourage his comrades.

Thomas L. Livermore, *Days and Events 1860-66.* (Boston: Houghton, Mifflin & Co., 1920).

**

Before the rebellion, John Brown Gordon had owned a number of coal mines in northern Georgia and southern Tennessee. When war erupted, he had raised a company of frontiersmen and backwoodsmen, characterized by their rough manner and even rougher clothing, including coonskin caps, buckskin clothing, and other rudimentary garments. As his native Georgia had enough troops to fill its regiments at the time, Gordon offered the services of his men to neighboring Alabama, whose governor accepted them and commissioned Gordon as a captain in the Sixth Alabama. He had since risen through the ranks to command the regiment, which was posted in the Sunken Road as a part of Rodes' Brigade. By September 1862, Colonel Gordon had developed quite a reputation for leading a charmed life. So many comrades had fallen at his side, so often had balls and shells pierced and torn his clothing, grazing his body without drawing a single drop of blood, that his men had come to believe that he was invincible. That reputation would be cemented in the "Bloody Lane."

Gordon was calmly talking with the commander of a North Carolina regiment, Col. Charles Tew, as a division of the Union II Corps approached their position. The first volley from the enemy lines sent a Minié ball through Tew's brain, killing him instantly, while another ball penetrated the calf of Gordon's right leg. On Gordon's left and right, his "men were falling under the death-dealing crossfire like trees in a hurricane." At relatively close rank, both sides exchanged a number of volleys, and firing became general. Gordon was struck a second time, higher up in the same leg, but still no bone was broken. He was able to hobble along the line and encourage his riflemen. Later in the day, a third bullet pierced his left arm, tearing asunder the tendons and mangling his flesh. When Gordon's men caught sight of the blood pouring down his coat sleeve, they pleaded for him to go to the rear; however, he refused to leave them during the crisis.

Soon after, a fourth ball ripped through his shoulder, leaving a wad of clothing in its track. Despite his painful wounds, Gordon could still stand and walk, although shock and the loss of blood had left him severely weakened. While hobbling a short distance down his line to steady a wavering position, he was shot down by a fifth bullet that struck Gordon squarely in the jaw, barely missing the jugular vein. He collapsed and lay unconscious in the dirt farm lane with his face buried in his cap. He might have smothered from the blood running into the cap, except that a Yankee, earlier in the contest, had shot a hole through the cap, which allowed the blood to drain out.

Colonel Gordon was carried to the rear lines and saved through the prompt actions of his surgeon. He was gradually nursed back to health by his wife, but would not see any more combat until the following year in the Gettysburg Campaign. He would finish the war as a corps commander under Lee, suffering other painful wounds and fulfilling his men's prediction that he indeed could not be killed by any Yankee bullet.

John B. Gordon, *Reminiscences of the Civil War.* (New York: Charles Scribner's Sons; Atlanta: Martin & Hoyt Co., 1904).

**

One enthusiastic woman, who followed the Federal "Irish Brigade" on the march as laundress or nurse, went into the fight at the Sunken Road with it. Standing near the field of battle, she repeatedly swung her bonnet in the air and cheered on the men. She emerged uninjured.

Thomas L. Livermore, *Days and Events 1860-66.* (Boston: Houghton, Mifflin & Co., 1920).

**

The courage of the unarmed woman was noteworthy, and stood in stark contrast to the behavior of a veteran colonel in the Irish Brigade. The trauma of war can have different psychological effects upon a man, even one with significant combat experience and a record of coolness under fire. As Maj. Charles Chipman of the Twenty-ninth Massachusetts led his regiment forward towards the Sunken Road, he noted "A Col. in our Brigade I saw lying under a hill while his Regt. was fighting nearly half a mile in front of him. He is now being tried for misbehavior before the enemy, but the best that you can make of war it is a horrid thing however necessary it may be at times." That cowering officer proved to be Col. John Burke of the Sixty-third New York, who had for some reason lagged behind his regiment, dismounted, and hid from enemy fire in a depression. He was subsequently court-martialed, cashiered from the army, and sent home in disgrace.

Charles Chipman papers, U.S. Army Military History Institute, Carlisle, Pennsylvania
Francis Walker, *History of the Second Army Corps.* (New York: Charles Scribner's Sons, 1887).

**

Emblematic of the carnage in the fields near the Sunken Road was the plight of the Sixty-third New York, bereft of their cowardly colonel. The regiment was cut down *en masse* attacking the Rebels in the Sunken Road. All but one of the field and line officers were struck down, and only fifty men were left by the end of the day, led by a captain. Sixteen separate soldiers fell while carrying the American flag, which was now in ribbons.

Report of Lt. Col. Henry Fowler, *The War of the Rebellion: A Compilation of the Official Records of the Union and Confederate Armies,* (Washington, D.C.: United States Government Printing Office, 1880-1901).

**

Among the Federal troops attacking the Sunken Road was the One Hundred and Thirty-second Pennsylvania. As it passed by William Roulette's modest farmhouse, a Rebel artillery shell exploded in his bee yard, freeing a large colony of honey bees that suddenly turned their anger on the most opportune target – the advancing Pennsylvanians. Soldiers already nervous from being under enemy artillery fire now had a fresh foe to face, and buzzing bees darted everywhere. Men dropped their weapons, batted and flailed at the attacking bees, rolled in the grass in an effort to escape the swarm, or ran off into Roulette's fields. Finally restoring order, the beleaguered regiment pressed forward at the double quick and soon ran into a swarm of angry Minié balls.

Files of the U.S. Army Medical Department, U.S. Army Military History Institute, Carlisle, Pennsylvania.

**

Assistant Surgeon George W. Hoover had joined the Thirty-second Pennsylvania's medical staff directly from medical school and had never even seen a gunshot wound until entering action that morning. His first patient was Capt. Robert A. Abbott, who staggered back to the regimental aid station after a bullet virtually removed his lower jaw. Sheltered from the massed volleys of enemy musketry only by a haystack, Dr. Hoover demonstrated remarkable courage and composure as he examined his first surgical patient and then saved him from drowning in his own blood by halting the hemorrhage via deft work with scalpel and sutures. Captain Abbott was but one of the 114 men wounded in the regiment on that morning as Surgeon Hoover became a veteran battlefield physician within a few hours as he worked tirelessly while under fire.

Files of the U.S. Army Medical Department, U.S. Army Military History Institute, Carlisle, Pennsylvania.

**

Daniel Harvey Hill was an experienced officer, but had a gruff personality that at times clashed with his peers, as well as with his superiors, including Robert E. Lee. Commanding a Confederate division at Antietam, the 41-year-old North Carolinian was riding in a small group of senior officers surveying the progress of the battle. Hidden from view behind the crest of a ridge, Lee and Longstreet dismounted to walk up to the crest to get a better view of enemy positions. General Hill, perhaps more impetuous than sensible, decided to stay on his horse. Longstreet remarked, "If you insist on riding up there and drawing the fire, give us a little interval, so that we may not be in the line of fire when they open upon you."

Lee and Longstreet were standing and surveying the Union lines through their field glasses when the latter spotted a puff of white smoke from a distant Federal cannon about a mile away. "There is a shot for you," he called out to the nearby Hill, who sat calmly on his horse during the three to four second interval as the ball whizzed towards the Confederate commanders. It struck Hill's horse and sheared off its front legs. The animal collapsed forward onto its bloody stumps, but remained standing on its intact hind legs, its croup (rump) high in the air and its head on the ground. A stunned D. H. Hill vainly tried to dismount, but was unable in several attempts to swing his leg over the elevated croup and his saddle roll. Finally Lee and Longstreet were able to help him get off the fallen animal, the third horse that Hill had had shot from under him thus far in the war.

An admiring Longstreet thought that it was the most accurate Yankee artillery shot he witnessed in the entire war.

Helen D. Longstreet, *Lee and Longstreet at High Tide.* (Gainesville, Georgia: self-published, 1904).

**

At least one man found his legs cowardly, though his heart may have been brave. During a crucial time in the fighting, he turned and made ready to run for the rear. A nearby officer in the Fifty-seventh New York realized the danger that, in such a critical situation, if one man were to break, all might follow. He sternly ordered the wavering man to lie down, but soon the shaken man rose and again started to the rear. Again, the officer ordered him to halt and lie down. This process was repeated a second time. The third time he arose, the officer threatened to shoot him if he stirred. By now, the bullets were flying thick and it was certain death to run. The wavering man assumed that it was safer to stay with the regiment and keep lying down than to get up and take off. However, he never forgot that humiliating Antietam battlefield incident. It seemed to rankle in his breast, and, months afterward, at winter camp in Falmouth, one night he came into his quarters half intoxicated. As he lay on his bunk, he kept muttering – first low, then louder and with a bitterer accent each time "Lie down," "*Lie down!*" "Lie down or I'll *shoot* you."

Gilbert Frederick, *The Story of a Regiment: Being the Military Service of the Fifty-Seventh New York State Infantry…* (New York: The Fifty-Seventh Veteran Association, 1857)

**

   In the throes of death and in agony from wounds, men sought places of refuge away from the scream of bullets. A number of injured Rebels were taken to the Henry Piper farmhouse, which was soon stripped of all muslin, linen, and calico cloth to bind up the wounded. After the battle, Union soldiers found three dead Confederates, one of which had crawled under Mrs. Piper's parlor piano to perish.

Pennsylvania at Antietam (Harrisburg: Harrisburg Publishing Company, 1907).

**

   A couple of times, Confederates tried to seize the guns of Battery A, First Rhode Island Artillery. A tall "rough-looking" Rebel, over six feet in height, approached the #4 gun with his steel bayonet fixed, intent on stabbing the lead crewman, who was distracted while sponging out the hot barrel. Spotting the Reb, he quickly ducked under the muzzle to protect himself from the flashing bayonet. One of the nearby infantrymen from the One Hundred and Thirty-second Pennsylvania, protecting the guns, was in the act of reloading his musket. He reversed the rifle and savagely clubbed the unsuspecting Confederate above the left ear, killing him. Brains splattered on the red-hot cannon barrel, where they "baked as quickly as if dropped on a hot stove." One of the gunnery sergeants later scraped them off with his knife and kept them as a gory trophy of Antietam.

Thomas M. Aldrich, *The History of Battery A, First Regiment Rhode Island Light Artillery in the War to Preserve the Union 1861-1865*. (Providence: Snow & Farnham, 1904)

**

   As one regiment was preparing for a second assault on an enemy position, the men had to pass through a piece of ground littered with the dead and dying from the unsuccessful prior attack. Although they were not yet under hostile fire, one soldier suddenly staggered amid the dead and dying, for he, to his sudden shock, had noted the body of his father, who belonged to a different regiment. Nearby lay a wounded man who knew both the father and son. He pointed to the still corpse and then upwards to the sky, and solemnly intoned, "It is well with him." Perhaps comforted by the thought that his father was now in Paradise, the young soldier regained his composure, fixed his bayonet, and rejoined the advance. After the battle, he returned and helped bury his father. He lovingly kept the only personal possession he found on his father's body, a Bible that had been given to him when he was an apprentice years before.

Frank Moore, *Anecdotes, Poetry, and Incidents of the War: North and South. 1860-1865.* (New York: Publication office, Bible house, J. Porteus, agent, 1867).

**

Men sometimes can get carried away with their emotions when exposed to the shock of war. Tears, cowardice, indifference, anger, arrogance, and recklessness can all be magnified in the trauma. Cpl. William Roach of the Eighty-first Pennsylvania took careful aim at a Confederate color sergeant as he retired and cleanly shot him, dropping the Rebel to the ground. Ignoring heavy musketry that continued along the opposing lines, Roach ran ahead of his company and lifted up the cap of the fallen flag bearer. He triumphantly placed the cap on the end of his bayonet and twirled it around, proudly exclaiming to his comrades in Company K, "*That* is the way to do it!" While he was absorbed in this self-congratulatory act of ego, another Union soldier slipped past, snatched up the fallen Confederate flag, and raced off brandishing the prize. Roach was left ruefully standing with only the Rebel cap.

Frank Moore, *Anecdotes, Poetry, and Incidents of the War: North and South. 1860-1865.* (New York: Publication office, Bible house, J. Porteus, agent, 1867).

**

The swirling action of the morning had steadily shifted southward. Maj. Gen. Ambrose Burnside was determined that his men should cross Antietam Creek and press on towards Sharpsburg. Due to a variety of factors, the main attack centered on the Lower (or Rohrbach) Bridge, one of three stone bridges crossing the creek along various roads leading towards the town. It was defended by a couple hundred Georgians ensconced on the bluffs just beyond the scenic bridge. Repeated Federal attempts to seize the crossing in the morning had failed. Burnside sent yet another brigade into action in the early afternoon.

Within this force was the Fifty-first Pennsylvania, a regiment smarting from recent disciplinary action by their colonel, Edward Ferrero. The teetotaler had punished his men by taking away a promised whiskey ration. He addressed his anxious men and the adjacent Fifty-first New York. "It is General Burnside's special request that the two Fifty-firsts take that bridge. Will you do it?" Cpl. Lewis Patterson remarked, "Will you give us our whiskey, Colonel, if we make it?" Ferrero thundered, "Yes, by God! You shall have as much as you want if you take that bridge," and ordered the advance. The two regiments stormed the bridge, New Yorkers to the left and Pennsylvanians to the right. They "charged up the road in column with fixed bayonets, and in scarcely more time than it takes to tell the bridge was passed." The men got their long anticipated whiskey a few days later.

Thomas H. Parker, *History of the 51ˢᵗ Regiment P.V. and V.V.* (Philadelphia: King & Baird, 1894).

**

As the fighting intensified around the Lower Bridge, the raucous racket of battle frightened a large sow and her litter. She raced directly towards the stunned Ninth New Hampshire, leaping over corpses that were in her way. She charged through a gap in a rail fence and then tried to run through the narrow opening between the legs of a soldier. He collapsed onto the back of the frightened hog, which carried him, screaming in terror, to the rear.

Edward O. Lord, *History of the Ninth Regiment New Hampshire Volunteers in the War of the Rebellion.* (Concord, New Hampshire: Republican Press Association, 1885).

**

Luck, training, location, and perhaps fate all play a role in combat survival. As the Seventh Ohio of Tyndale's Brigade in the XII Corps fought near the Dunker Church, Cpl. Edgar M. Condit was sighting his rifle when a sudden violent impact sent him sprawling to the ground. His jaw and face smarted from the unexpected blow. After examining himself to make sure he was okay, Condit rose to his feet. Recovering his rifle, he soon saw what had happened. A Rebel Minié ball was freshly lodged in his weapon's wooden stock. The impact had knocked him down, but the hard wood had blunted the force and saved him from being struck in the head and perhaps killed. In December, Condit was badly wounded in his left thigh during a battle at Dumfries, Virginia. As he was being loaded onto a stretcher, he entrusted the gun (still retaining the Antietam bullet firmly lodged in its stock) to a fellow soldier, remarking, "I would not exchange that gun for any 160 acres of land..." Unfortunately an enemy shell screamed into the group, and the gun with its souvenir leaden lump was tossed away as the men scrambled for safety.

Lawrence Wilson, *Itinerary of the Seventh Ohio Volunteer Infantry 1861-1864.* (New York and Washington: The Neale Publishing Company, 1907).

**

While the Confederate lines were being sorely pressed, Stonewall Jackson's Chief Surgeon, Hunter H. McGuire, rode out about 1:00 p.m. to find the eccentric general. Dr. McGuire was concerned that another Union attack might penetrate the thin patchwork Confederate line and overwhelm the Second Corps field hospital to the rear. He sought permission to move the wounded beyond the Potomac to Shepherdstown. McGuire found Jackson not far from the Dunker Church. Jackson was munching on a peach when McGuire approached him. The doctor remembered that he had his saddle pockets filled with peaches to take to the general, knowing how much he enjoyed fresh fruit. Before McGuire had a chance to explain the reason for his unexpected visit, Jackson anxiously asked if he had any more peaches. The doctor answered in the affirmative and told him yes, that he had indeed brought him some. After McGuire handed the general the peaches, he began to eat them ravenously, so much so, that he apologized and told the astonished doctor that he had had nothing to eat that day. Finally as Stonewall polished off the last of the delicacies, McGuire was able to interrupt Jackson's repast to explain his real reason for the trip to headquarters, and was granted the permission he sought.

Richmond Dispatch, July 19, 1891.

**

Col. William Irwin's brigade of the VI Corps Union reserve was sent into action in the early afternoon in a last effort to secure the Dunker Church area, which had changed hands several times the long day. One of Irwin's regiments, the Thirty-third New York, lost 46 men out of 150 effectives. When Confederate fire cut down most of the litter teams, Assistant Surgeon Richard J. Curran, a 24-year-old native of Ireland and a Harvard graduate, personally reorganized the survivors and led them in locating and retrieving the wounded. A recipient of the Medal of Honor for his conduct that day, Dr. Curran's citation noted how he "voluntarily exposed himself to great danger by going to the fighting line, there succoring the wounded and helpless and conducting them to the field hospital." A century after the war, Dr. Curran's heroic actions at Antietam inspired a postage stamp issued by the government of the African country of Sierra Leone.

Files of the U.S Army Medical Department, U.S. Army Military History Institute, Carlisle, Pennsylvania.

**

Another of Irwin's small regiments was the 181-man Seventh Maine, under the command of 24-year-old Maj. Thomas Hyde. One of the privates, an expert marksman named Knox, had been granted permission by Hyde to carry his own personal rifle into the battle. As the regiment laid prone dodging incoming Rebel artillery fire, Knox asked if he could take an advanced position to snipe at the enemy gunners. Every few minutes, the men could hear his rifle crack as one by one he picked off artillerymen who exposed themselves. After an hour of effective work, including shooting a horse from under a general who wandered into range with his staff, Knox carefully worked his way back to the major, carrying his trusted rifle, which had been ruined by a shell fragment that had struck the breech. Dismayed at the loss of his favorite weapon, but undaunted, Knox scooped up three regulation issue rifles from wounded Maine men and returned to his sniping.

Thomas W. Hyde, *Following the Greek Cross, or Memories of the Sixth Army Corps.* (Boston; Houghton, Mifflin and Co., 1894).

**

Vanity in combat can often be fatal, or, at least, quite painful. The acting adjutant of the Seventh Maine, William L. Haskell, rode his large horse "Old Whitey" into battle, making him more conspicuous to the soldiers (as well as to enemy marksmen). The eye-catching white charger soon tumbled with three bullets, one of which also slammed through both of Lieutenant Haskell's knees, incapacitating him.

Lewiston (Maine) *Journal*, October 2, 1862.

**

Instead of snapping off pistol shots at the Rebels, Swedish-born Col. Ernest Mathias Peter von Vegesack of the Twentieth New York was riding all around his rear line shooting skulkers from his mostly German regiment who refused to charge across the fields of the Mumma farm. The 42-year-old and highly volatile von Vegesack was no slouch when it came to combat. He would later receive the Medal of Honor for gallantry at Gaines' Mill during the Peninsula Campaign earlier that summer. A proud man, he was old school when it came to military affairs. At one point during the advance, Maj. Thomas Hyde of the adjacent Seventh Maine rode over to von Vegesack and asked him to lower the conspicuous regimental colors, as they were attracting considerable enemy fire. The crusty Swede tersely replied, "Let them wave; they are our glory!" The frustrated Hyde rode back to his regiment, which would lose over a third of its men during the day. He would finish his military service as a brigadier general, as would von Vegesack. For gallantry at Antietam, Major Hyde would later receive the Medal of Honor, one of twenty eventually awarded to veterans of the battle.

Thomas W. Hyde, *Following the Greek Cross, or Memories of the Sixth Army Corps.* (Boston; Houghton, Mifflin and Co., 1894).

**

Confederate Dr. Hunter McGuire, the Chief Surgeon of the Second Corps, was conversing in the mid-afternoon with Col. Andrew J. Grigsby, one of Stonewall Jackson's newer brigade commanders. The doctor noticed a large number of soldiers lying down in a distant field, and he supposed that it was an advanced line of battle. Surprised that these troops were so far away from the main Rebel force, he asked Grigsby why he did not move that line of battle to make it conform to his own. Grigsby grimly replied, "Those men you see lying over there, which you suppose to be a line of battle, are all dead men. They are Georgia soldiers."

Richmond Dispatch, July 19, 1891.

**

Having seen hard action throughout the Northern Virginia Campaign and now throughout the long day at Sharpsburg, several Confederate artillery batteries had run low on ammunition, and some had been withdrawn to the rear. Some enterprising crewmen of at least one depleted battery refused to give up firing at the distant enemy line. Soon, the Yankees were recoiling under a torrent of broken railroad iron, blacksmith's tools, hammers, and chisels. Some of these unusual incoming rounds had a peculiar sound, something akin to "which away, which way," that distinguished them from the regular shot and shell. When the Union soldiers heard this distinct noise, they would cry out, "Turkey! Turkey coming!" and would fall flat to avoid the scrap iron. One Union artillerist, a German, was startled by the tools raining around his battery and suddenly exclaimed, "My Got! We shall have the blacksmith's shop to come next!"

Frank Moore, *Anecdotes, Poetry, and Incidents of the War: North and South. 1860-1865.* (New York: Publication office, Bible house, J. Porteus, agent, 1867).

**

Not only were Confederate batteries running out of ammunition in parts of the field, they were also facing a scarcity of experienced artillerymen, as casualties had mounted. Capt. Merritt B. Miller of the famed Washington Artillery had withdrawn most of his battery to the rear to resupply their limbers and chests. Two guns remained firing from the Piper farm at the advancing Union lines near the Sunken Road, but the gun crews were eventually cut down by enemy sharpshooters. Lt. Gen. James Longstreet, hobbled by a badly blistered heel that forced him to go into battle wearing a carpet slipper on his bad foot, rode over to one of the abandoned guns. Chomping on a cigar, he quickly sized up the threat as waves of Union troops approached his position.

As the commander of the left wing of Lee's entire army later related, he pressed himself into service as a temporary artilleryman. "Our line was throbbing at every point, so that I dared not call on General Lee for help. Sergeant [William] Ellis thought that he could bring up ammunition if he was authorized to order it. He was authorized, and rode for and brought it. I held the horses of some of my staff who helped to man the guns as cannoneers." Longstreet directed the firing of the piece, which helped stem the growing blue tide.

James Longstreet, *From Manassas to Appomattox: Memoirs of the Civil War in America.* (Philadelphia: J. B. Lippincott Co., 1896).

**

Among the seemingly endless wave of Union attackers pressing towards the Piper Farm was the Fifth New Hampshire, commanded by Col. Edward E. Cross. The veteran officer always presented a fearsome appearance in combat – red-bearded, tall, and with a commanding stentorian voice that could readily be heard above the crackle of musketry. He had tied a red bandana around his bald head according to his custom, and his face was caked with a mixture of gunpowder and blood from a superficial scalp wound. He shouted to his men, "Put on war paint!" The soldiers responded, tearing open paper cartridges with their teeth and smearing black powder on their cheeks and foreheads. "Give 'em the war whoop!" exhorted Colonel Cross, and his men began screaming like Indians of old. Thomas Livermore later wrote, "All of us joined him in the Indian war whoop until it must have rung out above the thunder of the ordnance." He supposed this may have frightened the enemy, but he was sure Cross's impulsive act "reanimated us and let him know we were unterrified."

At Gettysburg the following summer, the normally combative Colonel Cross was convinced he would perish in the upcoming fight. He substituted a black bandana for his usual red one as he prepared for battle. His premonition came true, as he was indeed killed in action that afternoon.

Thomas L. Livermore, *Days and Events 1860-66.* (Boston: Houghton, Mifflin & Co., 1920).

**

Lt. Matthew Graham, Company H, Ninth New York, was in a field southeast of Sharpsburg waiting to go into action: "I was lying on my back, supported on my elbows, watching the shells explode overhead and speculating as to how long I could hold up my finger before it would be shot off, for the very air seemed full of bullets, when the order to get up was given, I turned over quickly to look at Col. Kimball, who had given the order, thinking he had become suddenly insane."

Matthew J. Graham, *The Ninth Regiment New York Volunteers (Hawkins' Zouaves)*... (New York: E. P. Copy & Co., 1900).

**

A New York correspondent sent the following back to his editor: "Some of the rebel missiles are military curiosities. One of the Hawkins Zouaves showed me a great big striped white marble that had hit him after it was spent from a cannon. Another soldier, a cultivated young man, known to literary friends of mine, told me of a comrade picking up the sheet iron plate of a door lock, all rolled up, key-hole perfect in it, no mistake, which had fallen near him from a rebel cannon. The key had probably been sent in another direction."

New York *Tribune*, September 22, 1863.

**

The Rebel artillerymen weren't the only ones hurling non-regulation ammunition at their targets. Pvt. George L. Kilmer of the Twenty-seventh New York later related that, as the battle raged, "A frenzy seized each man, and impatient with their small muzzle loaded guns, they tore the loaded ones from the hands of the dead and fired them with fearful rapidity, sending ramrods along with the bullets for double execution."

Files of the Antietam National Battlefield, National Park Service.

By mid-afternoon, the fighting had primarily shifted to the fields and woods southeast of Sharpsburg. D. R. "Neighbor" Jones' depleted division of Longstreet's command bore the brunt of an assault by part of the Federal IX Corps. Death and injury were commonplace, yet one particular incident stood out among the hundreds. One Fifteenth Georgia soldier later wrote, "I turned aside yesterday in the midst of the battle to see how a true soldier can die. He was of twenty-two or three summers — of clear skin and mild blue eyes — John S. Hudson, of Elbert County, Ga. His thigh had been torn off by a shell, and hung only by a thin piece of skin. He was calm and resigned, though his struggles were severe and protracted. Finally, as the dread hour of dissolution approached, he gathered up all his remaining strength and turning to his brother, who hung over in dumb agony, he said, 'Tell mother I die rejoicing and die a soldier's death.' There was not a dry eye among the dozen spectators who, strangely enough, had stopped to witness the last moments of the youthful hero. May Heaven have mercy upon his soul, and upon our bleeding land." Their young comrade now dead, the men of the Fifteenth quickly resumed their deadly work.

Southern Watchman, October 15, 1862.

**

Newton S. Manross, originally of Bristol, Connecticut, was an accomplished and learned man, a graduate of Harvard and a popular and successful college professor at Amherst College before the war. He had traveled abroad, studied at the University of Göttingen in Germany, and had completed his Ph.D. He was a world traveler, accomplished explorer, and frequent contributor to the scientific journals of the day. He had even invented a machine to cut crystals from the mineral calcspar.

Professor Manross was vacationing in his hometown of Bristol in August 1862 when the Sixteenth Connecticut was being recruited from among the gentry of that region. Making an impassioned speech to his fellow citizens, he had encouraged them to enlist and had been elected as their captain. As he departed for the infantry, he remarked to his wife, "You can better afford to have a country without a husband than a husband without a country."

He proved to be a worthy soldier, and his men loved him. However, Antietam was to be his first and last fight. The regiment had advanced into a rolling 40-acre cornfield south of Sharpsburg when the timely arrival of fresh Confederate troops under A.P. Hill halted their division's forward progress. When the battle was raging the fiercest, a shell fragment struck Captain Manross in the side and passed under his arm. A friend bending over him heard him softly murmuring, "Oh, my poor wife, my poor wife!" His death was universally mourned among the scientific community. A fellow professor lamented, "The world will never know its loss, but his friends will never forget theirs." Dr. Manross was only one of over 5,000 men whose lives and future contributions to society were cut short at Antietam.

B. F. Blakeslee, *History of the Sixteenth Connecticut Volunteers.* (Hartford: Case, Lockwood and Brainard Co., 1875).

**

Sgt. Joshua A. Armstrong, the color bearer of the Twenty-third Ohio, was a tall handsome lad who elicited the admiration (and perhaps a little jealousy) of his comrades for his "perfection of manly beauty." However, his courage and devotion to the national cause was unquestioned, although his height and daring made him a perfect target for Confederate riflemen. Shortly after the fighting at Crampton's Gap on South Mountain, Lt. Robert P. Kennedy was astonished to see Armstrong coming out of the fight still holding his banner. "Why Armstrong, I heard you were killed, you are not going to carry that banner still. I tell you no one can carry it and live." With a haughty scorn, Armstrong turned to the officer and exclaimed, "Then I'll carry it and die." Just a few days later at Antietam, that remark proved prophetic. A Rebel bullet pierced the banner and slammed into Armstrong's heart, and he fell entangled with the flag he so proudly had carried into the fight. Stained with Armstrong's blood, the torn and tattered colors of the Twenty-third would serve in other fights, and would proudly be displayed at veterans' reunions.

D. Cunningham and W. W. Miller, *Antietam: Report of the Ohio Battlefield Commission.* (Springfield, Ohio: Springfield Publishing Company, 1904).

**

By late-afternoon, Lee's defensive lines to the north and east of Sharpsburg were a patchwork of heavily depleted regiments and brigades. Thousands of men had become scattered from their own units. Brig. Gen. John B. Hood had pulled the battered remnants of his brigade to the rear, deploying his remaining men as skirmishers in an inverted V. Hood gave orders for his officers to collect all stragglers and shirkers, as well as any walking wounded (regardless of original organization or unit) and funnel them to the point of the V. Within a couple hours, he had assembled nearly 5,000 men, the vast majority of them not from his own division. According to Alabama infantryman J. S. Johnston, "It was, perhaps, an anomalous organization in warfare. No man knew any officer over him, nor even his file leader, or the man to the right or left of him. And thus was taken away every influence which gives men confidence and conduces to their greatest efficiency as soldiers."

Nevertheless, at 4 p.m., the order to "fall in" was heard and the stragglers marched towards the front lines as reinforcements. The men at the head of the column saw General Lee standing, with bared head and a "calm, but anxious expression," under the shade of an apple tree. As they passed by, he said, loud enough to be heard by several companies at a time, "Men, I want you to go back on the line, and show that *the stragglers* of the Army of Northern Virginia are *better than the best troops of the enemy.*" The effect, as may be imagined, was magnetic. The "Stragglers' Brigade," as it was afterwards called, was thrilled with enthusiasm. However, by the time the motley collection of troops reached the front lines, the battle had shifted to the south, and they were not needed. They dispersed and found their way back to their own regiments.

72

Rev. J. S. Johnston, "Reminiscences of Sharpsburg," *Southern Historical Society Papers*, Vol. VIII. (Richmond: Virginia, 1880).

**

By 4:00 p.m., fighting had essentially ceased north of Sharpsburg, except for the howling of occasional artillery shells. The Eighteenth Mississippi of Barksdale's Brigade was lying prone in an orchard about 600 yards from a stone wall sheltering the Union line. Sporadically, Federal shells would burst above the orchard and break off limbs from the fruit-laden trees. The famished Rebels "ate apples as long as we could swallow them."

James Dinkins, *1861-1865 by an Old Johnnie: Personal Recollections and Experiences in the Confederate Army.* (Cincinnati: The Robert Clarke Company, 1897).

**

On the Union side, a large number of regiments and batteries had only experienced cursory fighting, or had not been engaged at all – particularly in the V and VI corps. However, earlier in the day, many men in these corps had begun to prepare themselves mentally, as soldiers often do, for possible death. Col. Patrick R. Guiney of the Ninth Massachusetts in the V Corps had decked himself out in the morning with his brilliantly colorful dress sash. When one of his men reminded him that the eye-catching apparel might attract the attention of enemy sharpshooters, the Irish-born 27-year-old officer turned and gaily called out, "And wouldn't you have me a handsome corpse?" Both the men of the Ninth and the nearby Thirty-second Massachusetts roared with laughter, the tension now broken. For much of the day, they would be spectators to the fury of Antietam. The dapper Guiney would survive the war (although he suffered a nasty wound to his left eye in the Wilderness) to unsuccessfully run for Congress. He died at the age of 42 as a result of his Civil War wound. There is no record if indeed he made a handsome corpse.

Francis J. Parker, *The Story of the Thirty-second Regiment, Massachusetts Infantry.* (Boston: C. W. Calkins, 1880).

**

As the IX Corps rallied after A. P. Hill's surprise attack and reformed, its brigades maintained their battle lines into the early evening. Sporadic firing, sometimes heavy, continued well into the evening, making duty on the frontlines hazardous. The Sixth New Hampshire was engaged in a warm small arms duel with distant Rebels, with men from both sides sheltered behind logs, trees, or anything else that might cover their heads while they were reloading their muskets. Sgt. William W. French of Company B was behind a tree, loading and firing as fast as he possibly could at furtive targets three to four hundred yards away. Sgt. Howard Rand of Company K slipped behind French and requested that he step back and load both his and Rand's rifles, and allow Rand, a "good shot" in his own mind, to have a crack at the Rebels. French consented, withdrew down the slope, loaded the muskets, and passed one up to Rand, who had since taken his place behind the tree.

Carelessly, Rand stepped to one side of the tree to get a better view of his target. However, the Reb was too quick for Rand and drilled him cleanly in the forehead with a bullet, killing him almost instantly. Rand's lifeless corpse tumbled downhill, collecting French in the process. Both rolled partway down the slope. French pushed aside Rand's body and made his way back to his tree, where he was careful not to allow the "Johnnies" to get the first shot at him.

Capt. Lyman Jackman, *History of the Sixth New Hampshire Regiment in the War for the Union.* (Concord, New Hampshire: Republican Press Association, 1891).

**

Death and injury in battle did not always directly come from bullets and flying shell fragments, and it did not always happen on the front lines. Levi P. Dodge, a 23-year-old hospital steward in the rear lines of the Sixth New Hampshire, was badly injured by a fractious horse at Antietam. Being slow to recover from his injuries, he was mustered out of the army on medical disability in January 1863 and sent home. When he finally recovered, he enrolled in medical school and became a doctor, as later did his two sons.

Granville P. Conn, *History of the New Hampshire Surgeons in the War of the Rebellion.* (Concord, New Hampshire: Ira C. Evans Co., 1906).

**

The men of the Twenty-third Ohio were surprised and pleased to see their regimental commissary sergeant frequently risk personal safety to bring them roasted meat and hot coffee with a mule-drawn wagon, at times ducking as Rebel bullets whizzed by. After the war, that propensity to aid others served the courageous sergeant well. He was William McKinley, destined to be the twenty-fifth President of the United States. For his courage under fire at Antietam, he was promoted to second lieutenant by his commanding officer, another future President from Ohio, Rutherford B. Hayes.

D. Cunningham and W. W. Miller, *Antietam: Report of the Ohio Battlefield Commission.* (Springfield, Ohio: Springfield Publishing Company, 1904).

**

The sights and scenes of America's bloodiest day were never to be forgotten. Pvt. David Thompson of the Ninth New York noted that when some his comrades in Company G went to the rear for water, they discovered the charred remains of several Confederates in the ashes of some hay ricks that had been set on fire by Union shells.

David L. Thompson, "In the Ranks to the Antietam," *Battles and Leaders of the Civil War*, Volume II. (New York: The Century Co., 1887-88).

**

Although some Federal units had not even fired a shot, losses had been ghastly for many regiments on both sides. Shattered regiments reformed and checked muster rolls to see who was still present. The Seventeenth Virginia in Kemper's Brigade, for example, went into the battle with only fifty-five healthy men, 46 enlisted men and 9 officers. It was already much depleted from severe losses during the Northern Virginia Campaign. Now, only 16 remained uninjured, 2 of them prisoners of war, including Alex Hunter. Few of the wounded had kept back any of the apple brandy that Hunter and the foragers had purloined from the dairy loft two days before.

Alexander Hunter, *Johnny Reb and Billy Yank*. (New York and Washington: The Neale Publishing Company, 1905).

**

Thousands of men lay dead, dying, or wounded in the fields and woods around Sharpsburg. Lt. John S. Mosby, who would later be famed as the "Gray Ghost" for his partisan exploits, toured the battlefield looking for General Stuart. Of the hundreds of stricken men who were lying all around him, Mosby's attention was in some way attracted to a wounded officer who was lying in an uncomfortable position and seemed to be suffering great agony. He dismounted, rearranged the wounded man more comfortably, and rolled up a blanket and placed it under the man's head. The cavalier procured a canteen of water from the body of a dead soldier lying nearby. As he returned to the fallen officer, Mosby passed by another wounded soldier. He paused and held the canteen to him so that he could drink. The enlisted man astonished Mosby with his sincere remark, "No, take it to my Colonel; he is the best man in the world." Despite his own painful wound, chivalry and unselfishness were the hallmarks of this unknown common infantryman.

John S. Mosby, *The Memoirs of Colonel John S. Mosby*. (Boston: Little, Brown, and Company, 1917).

**

Hundreds of soldiers had been killed outright. Thousands more were mortally wounded and suffered through slow, agonizing deaths. At least one soldier chose suicide over a prolonged painful demise. Young Pvt. Milford N. Bullock of the Thirty-fourth New York was dying from a severe wound that was causing tremendous pain and unbearable suffering. Lying on his back, the Herkimer County native placed the muzzle of his loaded rifle to his head and manipulated his ramrod to pull the trigger. His comrades in Company K found him after the battle. They were so shook up about the event that they unanimously agreed not to write home with particulars about the incident in fear that Bullock's family would find out the true circumstances of his death. It was not until 40 years later at an Antietam reunion that the story was finally told publicly.

Lewis N. Chapin, *A Brief History of the Thirty-fourth Regiment N.Y.S.V.* (New York: Regimental Monument Commission, 1903?).

**

Late in the afternoon and into the early evening, U.S. Army Surgeon James L. Dunn was desperate for bandages and dressing for wounds, as casualties flooded into his brigade's field hospital established on the Poffenberger farm behind Union lines. The Pennsylvanian had "expended every bandage, torn up every sheet in the house, and everything we could find." To his relief, he noted the arrival of a covered wagon carrying an old acquaintance, Clara Barton. The forty-year-old nurse had arrived from Washington as soon as she could, with a wagon loaded down with all kinds of material for dressing wounds, as well as other supplies the surgeons and stewards would need. She distributed her load among the various field hospitals and spent all night and the next couple of days making soup to nourish the wounded. When Dunn left four days later, he noted that Barton was still hard at work. To his amazement and delight, upon his return a week later, she was still tirelessly ministering to the needs of the wounded and dying, "all out of her own private fortune," according to the doctor. Dunn later remarked, "In my feeble estimation, Gen. McClellan, with all his laurels, sinks into insignificance beside the true heroine of the age – *the angel of the battle-field.*"

Frank Moore, *Anecdotes, Poetry, and Incidents of the War: North and South. 1860-1865.* (New York: Publication office, Bible house, J. Porteus, agent, 1867).

**

Even the rear lines were not entirely safe from the flying missiles of death. Nurse Clara Barton stooped to give a drink to a wounded man lying upon the ground. She gingerly raised his head with her right hand and held the cup to his lips with her other hand. She felt a sudden twitch of the loose sleeve of her dress, and immediately the poor fellow sprang from her hands and fell back quivering in the agonies of death. A stray bullet had passed between her body and her right arm that supported the soldier, cutting through her sleeve and passing through his chest from shoulder to shoulder.

Files of the Antietam National Battlefield, National Park Service.

**

One of the many patients treated by Clara Barton was a soft-faced young soldier who had been shot in the chest. When Barton examined the wound, she discovered that the "boy" was actually a girl. Barton gently coaxed the disguised female to reveal her true identity, Mary Galloway, and then convinced her to go back home to recuperate. Galloway had enlisted to be with her husband. A few other women also fought at Antietam in the guise of men.

National Archives and Records Administration

**

Maj. William Capers White of the Seventh South Carolina was among the thousands of victims of Antietam. As Kershaw's Brigade swept forward past Dunker Church, White was knocked to the ground by the concussion from a shell bursting overhead. Rising and wiping off the dust and blood, he pushed his men forward towards a distant abandoned Yankee battery. Struck in the face by a bullet, he pressed forward, ignoring the pain. Seeing that the guns were being re-crewed, he rushed ahead to within twenty yards of the enemy. However, the gunners managed to get off a round of canister before the Confederates arrived and White was killed instantly with a ball in his skull.

One of his captains later wrote, "One of the most touching things I have seen since my connection with the army, was the devotion of Major White's servant, an old negro he brought from home with him. The Major was shot at a battery which we charged, and from which we were obliged, from lack of support, to fall back. The news had not reached the old man, and the next morning he rode down to the lines where we were, to bring the Major's breakfast; and when he learned that the Major was dead he sat down and wept like a child. After recovering himself he begged to go to the enemy's lines and try and recover his master's body, and when refused, his grief seemed to increase tenfold. All day he watched and waited, hoping by some means to get the body; and when I insisted that he should go to the rear, the old man left very reluctantly, begging me to use every means to recover his master's remains. The next morning he saddled his horse, packed all the master's baggage upon him, and started off on his homeward journey of nearly a thousand miles. An instance of greater devotion I never saw."

Charleston *Mercury*, December 3, 1862.

Chapter 4

The Aftermath

Thursday, September 18, 1862

Several Rebels spent the morning shooting stray livestock for breakfast, eagerly killing chickens, cows, and geese. Prussian-born Heros von Borcke, long a favorite of J.E.B. Stuart, watched one of Hood's Texans carefully aim at a frightened pig galloping down a street some sixty yards away. He dropped it in its tracks. An admiring Von Borcke thought it was a "capital shot," but, as an officer, he was compelled to rebuke the soldier for his wanton disregard of the order banning the destruction of private property. Stunned at the unexpected rebuke, the lanky Texan inquired, "Major, did you have anything to eat yesterday?" He ruefully added, "I haven't tasted a morsel in days." A sympathetic von Borcke allowed the man to collect the slain pig and take it back for his company's meal.

Heros von Borcke, *Memoirs of the Confederate War for Independence*. (New York: Peter Smith, 1938).

**

Skirmishing continued throughout the morning, although neither commanding general was in the mood to renew the bloody hostilities. Still, death was the destiny for several soldiers who had survived America's bloodiest day. One member of the Seventh Virginia had gone forward to help remove Union wounded from the regiment's front. As he was helping a stricken Yankee, he was shot through the body and killed by a hidden Federal sharpshooter, who was so far away that the report from his rifle could not even be heard by the rest of the men engaged in removing the wounded.

David E. Johnston, *The Story of a Confederate Boy in the Civil War*. (Portland, Oregon: Glass & Prudhomme Company, 1914).

**

While the Union and Confederate soldiers often expended tremendous energy and passion in killing one another, there were ties that often bound them together beyond their status as mortal enemies. Early in the morning, the Fifth New Hampshire was on picket duty in the middle of a cornfield near the Sunken Road. Confederate sharpshooters were keeping up a hot fire on anyone who dared expose himself. Just outside of the picket line lying among the cornstalks was a badly wounded Rebel, who called for assistance. One of the New Hampshire men worked his way to him and was handed a slip of paper. The stricken Confederate had used a stick wetted with blood to scrawl a circle with a few mystic signs inside, and now he begged the Yankee to take the note to some Freemason as soon as possible.

The Yank slipped back to the main line concealed in a field behind the corn and handed the paper to Col. Edward E. Cross, a known Master Mason. However, Cross could not interpret the strange symbols and correctly assumed they belonged to a higher order. He showed the bloody inscription to one of his captains, J. B. Perry, who was a Thirty-second Degree Mason. Perry replied that a brother Mason was in peril, and immediately Cross organized a party of four soldiers to rescue the fallen man. They stealthily crawled through the corn to avoid the attention of the watchful sharpshooters, found the Mason, and placed him on a blanket. At great risk to themselves, they carried him out of rifle range to the Fifth's field hospital in the rear.

The enemy soldier, suffering from severe wounds to his thigh and chest, turned out to be Lieutenant Edon of an Alabama regiment. He might have bled to death had it not been for Cross's order and the bravery of the Union soldiers who risked their own lives to save a Rebel. A grateful Edon mentioned that another wounded Mason was also laying nearby, a lieutenant colonel of a Georgia regiment. Likewise, Union soldiers returned to the edge of the dangerous cornfield to also bring him back to the medical station. A "warm friendship" soon emerged between the wounded officers, both blue and gray, in the hospital.

Frank Moore, *Anecdotes, Poetry, and Incidents of the War: North and South. 1860-1865.* (New York: Publication office, Bible house, J. Porteus, agent, 1867).

**

On the front lines, many men in the skirmish lines had finally had enough of the continued killing. On Lee's left flank, pickets from Stonewall Jackson's shattered corps had been exchanging fire with Federal skirmishers for some time at relatively close range. Finally, one enterprising Rebel called out to his opponent across the field and asked him not to shoot, to which the Yankee assented. However, bullets still whizzed through the air. Soon afterwards, the exasperated Confederate shouted, "Say Yank, tell the man to your left not to shoot; I would just as lief (soon) be shot by you as by him." Word was soon passed from man to man along both lines in the sector, and the guns fell quiet.

Ben La Bree, *Camp Fires of the Confederacy: A Volume of Humorous Anecdotes, Reminiscences, Deeds of Heroism,...* (Louisville, Kentucky: The Courier-Journal Job Printing Company, 1898).

**

For much of the day, the opposing armies stood in line of battle grimly contemplating each other, neither one anxious to renew the bloody engagement. Under a flag of truce, unarmed parties scurried about picking up the wounded that lay exposed between the lines. The Confederate ambulance corpsmen, with pieces of white cloth on their hats, and Federal soldiers with white bands tied around their arms, mixed freely on the field. The shell-scarred Dunker Church soon became a focal point of the fraternization. At one point, some muskets were fired, whether by accident or design, and in an instant each army sprang into line, cannoneers in position, and all ready at once to renew the combat. Fortunately, it proved to be a false alarm, and neither side reopened the hostilities.

Harper's Weekly, October 25, 1862.

**

Charles Coffin, the intrepid reporter of the Boston *Journal* who had roamed all over the battlefield, rode over to the Dunker Church to mingle with the gaggle of socializing soldiers. He recalled, "Nearby stood a wounded battery-horse and a shattered caisson belonging to one of Hood's batteries. The animal had eaten every blade of grass within reach. No human being ever looked more imploringly for help than that dumb animal, wounded beyond the possibility of moving, yet resolutely standing, as if knowing that lying down would be the end."

Charles C. Coffin, "Antietam Scenes," *Battles and Leaders of the Civil War*, Volume II. (New York: The Century Co., 1887-88).

**

Among the thousands of dead was Pvt. Joseph Wright of the Seventh South Carolina, who had been killed during General Kershaw's counterattack on the Union II Corps. He was one of *nine* sons of Jacob Wright of Edgefield, South Carolina, that had enlisted in the Confederate Army. Three of the brothers were killed during the Civil War, three severely wounded, and three emerged from the war unhurt.

Confederate Veteran, 1913, page 8.

**

Pvt. John Conline of the Fourth Vermont went sightseeing during the morning. He noted the stiff body of a Confederate who had been shot and killed while trying to escape to the rear across a rail fence on the west side of the Sunken Road. The rigid Rebel was transfixed in death in an erect position, with his right foot across the rail and his left in a partial kneeling position. One hand was holding a piece of apple in his mouth, the last food he would ever taste on earth. Conline counted seven bullet holes in his back.

John Conline, *Recollections of the Battle of Antietam and the Maryland Campaign*. (Detroit: Stone Printing Company, 1898).

**

Lt. Thomas Jefferson Spurr of the Fifteenth Massachusetts had been badly wounded in the thigh during the savage fighting in the West Woods. Like the majority of the immobile Union wounded, he had been left behind when Sedgwick's division of the II Corps had retreated. Weakened by blood loss and shock, the pre-war lawyer had suffered alone in agony throughout the long night. The area where he lay was now occupied by Confederates. An officer of a South Carolina regiment happened by the stricken Spurr on Thursday and recognized him as an old college pal from their days at Harvard. They had not seen each other in the four years since they graduated. The bonds of past personal friendship easily overcame the differing colors of their uniforms, and the Rebel compassionately knelt beside his old friend and ministered to him. He shouldered the wounded New Englander and carried him to a nearby farm yard pressed into service as a Confederate field hospital.

The 24-year-old Spurr was placed near a couple of haystacks and covered with a blanket. For two days, he stayed put as doctors stabilized him enough to prepare him for transport to a hospital in Hagerstown. He lived long enough for his mother Mary to travel from Massachusetts to visit him one last time before he passed away a few days later on September 27. He was only one of forty-three injured men of his regiment and its attached sharpshooter company who died before Christmas from their wounds. Another seventy-four had died on the battlefield, marking the Fifteenth Massachusetts as one of the most devastated regiments in the Federal army at Antietam.

Andrew E. Ford, *The Story of the Fifteenth Regiment Massachusetts Volunteer Infantry in the Civil War 1861-1864.* (Clinton, Massachusetts: Press of W. J. Coulter, 1898). Names inscribed on the base of the Fifteenth Massachusetts lion monument, Antietam National Battlefield.

**

Not all the battlefield burials had been completed when the temporary armistice between the armies expired at 5 p.m. As a burial party from the Twenty-seventh New York was still collecting the dead, without warning, they were suddenly fired upon by nearby Rebels. Five unsuspecting stretcher bearers were cut down and wounded, and seven more surrendered as prisoners of war. An angry Maj. Gen. Henry Slocum, commander of the Union Twelfth Corps, quickly dispatched his assistant adjutant general, Maj. Hiram C. Rogers, under a white flag through the Rebel lines to meet with General Lee's staff. The truce was extended until the next morning to avoid more senseless shooting.

Charles B. Fairchild, *History of the 27th Regiment, N.Y. Vols.* (Binghamton, New York: Carl & Matthews, 1888).

**

Before the sunlight faded, Pvt. David Thompson of the Ninth New York walked over the narrow field. "All around lay the Confederate dead...clad in 'butternut'...As I looked down on the poor pinched faces...all enmity died out. There was no 'secession' in those rigid forms nor in those fixed eyes staring at the sky. Clearly it was not their war."

David L. Thompson, "In the Ranks to the Antietam," *Battles and Leaders of the Civil War*, Volume II. (New York: The Century Co., 1887-88).

**

Charles Carlton Coffin, the roving *Boston Journal* correspondent, later wrote of Antietam, "I recall a Union soldier lying near the Dunker Church with his face turned upward, and his pocket Bible open upon his breast. I lifted the volume and read the words: 'Though I walk through the valley of the shadow of death, I will fear no evil; for thou art with me. Thy rod and thy staff, they comfort me.' Upon the fly-leaf were the words, 'We hope and pray that you may be permitted by kind Providence, after the war is over, to return.'"

Charles C. Coffin, "Antietam Scenes," *Battles and Leaders of the Civil War*, Volume II. (New York: The Century Co., 1887-88).

**

During the rainy, damp Thursday night, Lee's battered army quietly retired from Sharpsburg and began crossing the Potomac River into Virginia, most using Packhorse (Boteler's) Ford near Shepherdstown. As Confederate cavalry under Col. Thomas T. Munford reached the riverbank, he encountered Brig. Gen Maxcy Gregg with about one hundred men, the rear guard of the infantry. Just beyond the edge of the river in the chilly water stood an ambulance filled with wounded men. The cowardly driver had unhitched his horses, crossed the river on foot, and had left his suffering comrades to the mercy of the foe. The poor injured fellows begged piteously to be carried to the other side. General Gregg lifted his hat, and said to his South Carolinians, "My men, it is a shame to leave these poor fellows here in the water! Can't you take them over the river?" In an instant, a dozen or more strong men laid hold of the heavy ambulance and pulled it through the water, in most places waist deep, amid the shouts of the rest, who lustily sang "Carry me back to Old Virginia."

Henry B. McClellan, *The Life and Campaigns of Major-General J.E.B. Stuart.* (Boston: Houghton, Mifflin & Co., 1885).

**

Just before leaving Sharpsburg, Capt. George F. Norton of the First Virginia detailed Cpl. Lawrence Carroll and six men to fill the company's canteens with water. On his way to find a source of potable water, Carroll spied an inviting warehouse where whiskey was being stored. Putting on an air of authority, he marched his detail up to the building and "officially" relieved its Georgia guards. As soon as they were out of sight, his men filled the empty canteens with good Maryland whiskey. Soon, Company C was tipsy from the canteens' contents, "which caused the step of most of the men to be rather uncertain in fording the stream." The tipsy Virginians made it into Shepherdstown without further incident.

Charles T. Loehr, *War History of the Old First Virginia Infantry Regiment, Army of Northern Virginia.* (Richmond: Wm. Ellis Jones, 1884).

**

Among the last to cross the Potomac River were J.E.B. Stuart's veteran cavalry troopers, who maintained a desultory fire with Yankee pursuers. Late at night, Gen. Wade Hampton led his brigade across the Potomac between Falling Waters and Sharpsburg at an "old blind ford." It was a harrowing crossing. One moment standing on rocks half leg deep in the cold water, the next step would plunge both horse and rider up to the neck. A shivering Pvt. Wiley Howard of the Cobb Legion finally fell asleep a while before daybreak, lying on a rock pile with his clothes soaking wet. He later recalled, "Oh! How delicious to be thus allowed to sleep, wet and hungry, while I dreamed of a soft downy feather bed away at home." Dreams and memories of home often were all that sustained the Civil War soldier.

Wiley C. Howard, *Sketch of Cobb Legion Cavalry and Some Incidents and Scenes Remembered.* (Speech read before the United Confederate Veterans Camp #159 in Atlanta, Georgia, August 19, 1901).

**

Competition between regiments was frequent, whether it was on the ball field, battlefield, or on the march. During the withdrawal from Sharpsburg, Kemper's Brigade, led by the much depleted Seventeenth Virginia under Maj. Arthur Herbert, had been ordered to follow Drayton's Brigade. In the darkness and confusion following the river crossing, the Seventeenth had lost sight of Drayton's rear echelons. Hurrying forward in an effort to catch up to them, the Virginians had to pass through a narrow ravine, just wide enough to allow one regiment to pass four men abreast. At its entrance, Kemper's men encountered the Fifth North Carolina, coming from another direction at the same time and also aiming to enter the same ravine. Major Herbert calmly explained to the commander of the Tar Heels that he had to go first, as the brigade had been ordered to immediately follow Drayton's men.

The North Carolina officer paid no heed and ordered his regiment into the narrow passageway. Herbert, a wealthy Alexandria banker, suddenly sang out, "Forward Seventeenth!" and the competition became heated as the two combative regiments jostled for position. Cries of "Forward Fifth" and "Forward Seventeenth" alternately rent the night air. Soon, they were accompanied by the booming voice of Capt. Robert M. Mitchell, commanding the Eleventh Virginia next in line in Kemper's column – "Forward men, follow the old Seventeenth, and don't let them get between you." The column of Virginians finally won the tussle, passing triumphantly through the ravine. The dismayed men of the Fifth North Carolina were jammed against the steep rocky sides of the gorge or had to clamber halfway up the hillside and hold onto roots to avoid falling into the passing soldiers underneath. The boys from the Old Dominion State celebrated their triumph with a shout and then taunted the defeated Tar Heels with "Come along Fifth?"

83

George Wise, *History of the Seventeenth Virginia Infantry.* (Baltimore: Kelly, Piet & Company, 1870).

Friday, September 19, 1862

Across the now quiet battlefield of Antietam, soldiers looked for their fallen comrades, and burial parties began the grim task of interring the thousands of bodies. Images of mangled corpses and the stench of rotting flesh abounded. In a small clump of woods, one dead Union soldier was found in an upright position, peacefully leaning against a tree. According to one eyewitness, "The expression of the man's countenance was perfectly natural – in fact he appeared as if he was only asleep. Alongside of him was an old and worn Bible, which the poor fellow, knowing his time had come, was reading, and in this way, a soldier and Christian, he died..." Like most of the other dead, he was buried in an unmarked grave.

Frank Moore, *Anecdotes, Poetry, and Incidents of the War: North and South. 1860-1865.* (New York: Publication office, Bible house, J. Porteus, agent, 1867).

**

Most of the Confederate dead were hastily buried in large pits or trenches, often marked with simple wooden signs on which had been written such messages as, "87 Rebels are buried in this hole," "Here lie 60 Rebels," etc. Sometimes, these crude markers carried other epitaphs from sarcastic or vengeful Yankee gravediggers, including "The wages of sin is death," "Here lies a poor dead fool; he fought for his right to the soil, and now he has obtained it," and, regarding one particular Southern officer, "He lied well while living; he seems to lie well while dead."

Henry C. Morhous, *Reminiscences of the 123rd Regiment, N.Y.S.V.* (Greenwich, New York: People's Journal Book and Job Office, 1879).

**

Souvenir hunting was a common pastime now that the shooting had stopped. Sgt. Nathan Dykeman of the One Hundred and Seventh New York ducked into the shell-scarred Dunker Church, where he spotted the leather-bound Bible used by the congregation. He walked out with it and arranged to have it sent home. It stayed in his house in Schuyler County, New York, until 1903 when his sister sold it to the regimental veterans' organization. After a roundabout path, it finally ended up in the possession of the National Park Service and is now on display at the Antietam National Battlefield's Visitors Center.

Files of the Antietam National Battlefield, National Park Service.

**

As Capt. George Noyes and some New York comrades traipsed the battlefield, they were horrified by the carnage of war – particularly the torn, mutilated, and mangled bodies of the dead. However, to their surprise, near some haystacks in a field not far from the turnpike they encountered "the only pleasing picture on this battlefield, a majestic and serene horse which apparently had died while struggling to rise from his fatal wound. His head was half lifted, his neck proudly arched; every muscle seemed replete with animal life." His death wound was concealed from view, so Noyes had to ride up and inspect the animal to make sure he was really dead. (Author's note: This same dead horse was photographed a few days after the battle by Alexander Gardner. It most likely belonged to Col. Henry Strong of the Sixth Louisiana, who also perished in the brutal morning phase of the battle.)

George F. Noyes, *The Bivouac and the Battle-Field; or, Campaign Sketches in Virginia and Maryland* (New York: Harper & Brothers, 1863)

**

One raw recruit in the Fifth New York, a soldier only a week, wandered off from his regiment in the days after the battle "to discover what was new." In his rambles, he happened upon a large house with an inviting open window. With the curiosity of youth, he walked over to it and raised his head above the sill. He was startled as the gory stump of a human arm was suddenly thrust in his face, and a voice from inside the house commanded, "Young man, take this away and bury it!" The recruit walked back to his regiment sick to his stomach, for he had unknowingly stumbled across one of the many homes that had been converted into field hospitals. Wiser for his efforts, he did no more sightseeing at Antietam.

Alfred Davenport, *Camp and Field Life of the Fifth New York Volunteer Infantry: (Duryee Zouaves).* (New York: Dick and Fitzgerald, 1879).

**

The fighting at Sharpsburg was not quite over, although the shooting had finally stopped. Pvt. Alexander Hunter of the Seventeenth Virginia and other prisoners of war had been herded to the rear of the Union lines, where they awaited disposition and possible parole. The barefooted Hunter was dressed only in a badly torn, threadbare gray jacket and some patched captured blue pants he had picked up on an earlier battlefield. He could not help but notice his captors' comfortable uniforms, complete with underwear, a commodity he no longer enjoyed. Soon, he and a number of other uninjured Rebels were escorted into Sharpsburg to fetch water for their compatriots.

The town's water pumps were a coveted commodity. As Union soldiers and Confederate prisoners jostled for position to fill their canteens, Hunter shoved aside a Yankee, who swiftly retaliated by punching the prisoner. The Virginian proceeded to knock his canteen over the Federal's head. "Fight!" gleefully roared the onlookers.

85

Quickly the crowd, blue and gray alike, formed a ring and shoved the two combatants inside. One big, brawny Yank patted the scrawny Rebel on the back and promised him, as a West Virginian, that he would ensure a fair fight, so "go in and win." Just as the two fighters were about to come to blows, a Union officer, seeing the commotion by the town pump, rode up and dispersed the crowd, which walked away grumbling that their entertainment had been halted. Alex Hunter was "always thankful that officer came along, for he saved my bones a severe rattling."

Alexander Hunter, *Johnny Reb and Billy Yank.* (New York and Washington: The Neale Publishing Company, 1905).

**

Wilder Dwight, Lt. Colonel of the Second Massachusetts, had been an honors graduate from Harvard and a pre-war lawyer. He had been captured at Winchester earlier in the year while advancing alone to help a wounded soldier. Paroled just before the Maryland Campaign, he had hustled to Damascus, Maryland, where he rejoined his regiment. Mortally wounded in the fighting at Antietam, the 29-year-old officer lingered until September 19, when he summoned enough strength to open his eyes and say a few last words to a chaplain bending over him, "It is all right, Mr. Chaplain, I know that I am done for; but I want you to understand that I don't flinch a hair. I *should* like to live a few days, so as to see my father and mother… But, apart from that, if God calls for me this minute, I am ready to go." Dwight was buried in Brookline, Massachusetts, with six companies of the Forty-fourth Massachusetts providing the honor guard.

Two days earlier, Dwight had just enough time to quickly scrawl what would be his last brief letter home:

Near Sharpsburg, September 17, 1862. On the field.
Dear Mother,

It is a misty, moisty morning; we are engaging the enemy, and are drawn up in support of Hooker, who is now banging away most briskly. I write in the saddle, to send you my love, and to say that I am very well so far.

Alonzo H. Quint, *The Record of the Second Massachusetts Infantry 1861-1865.* (Boston: James P. Walker, 1867).
Wilder Dwight (posthumous), *Life and Letters of Wilder Dwight.* (Boston: Ticknor and Fields, 1868).

Saturday, September 20, 1862 and beyond

Often in war, misunderstanding and misperceptions can color a person's opinion of his fellow soldiers. At times, this can lead to contempt and resentment. These feelings can be individual or collective. There were incidents in the Civil War that led

86

entire regiments (or brigades in some cases) to mistrust and even hate one another, sometimes even more than hating the enemy. One such incident occurred at the Battle of Shepherdstown on September 20. General McClellan had directed part of the V Corps under Fitz John Porter to cross the Potomac at Packhorse Ford near Shepherdstown, Virginia. This two-brigade force was to reconnoiter the southern side of the river and ascertain the whereabouts of Lee's rear guard, but was not to bring about a general engagement. They moved up a narrow road past Boteler's Mill and lay prone in a field while artillery shells whizzed overhead at A.P. Hill's Rebels, who had quickly returned to the ford to repel the Union forces.

     As one of Hill's brigades emerged from the woods, they struck the right of the Union defensive line, which was held by a newly recruited regiment, the One Hundred and Eighteenth Pennsylvania. Raised and equipped by the Philadelphia Corn Exchange (a commodities trading house), the regiment had been in the service only twenty days, and were crushed by an oblique attack, sending them tumbling to the rear. The veteran Twenty-second Massachusetts was farther upriver during this sudden attack, still struggling to wade across the deeper part of the Potomac. The brigade commander, James Barnes, had issued orders for the regiments to withdraw, which the Twenty-second obeyed. However, the order had not reached the Pennsylvanians' commander with the proper line of communications, so that regiment had stayed put and absorbed the brunt of the Confederate attack alone and unsupported. As the Twenty-second had successfully withdrawn, a rift occurred between them and the surviving Pennsylvanians over the incident, one which would never be mended, even long after the war.

John L. Parker and Robert G. Carter, *History of the Twenty-second Massachusetts Volunteer Infantry...* (Boston, 1887).

**

     War can bring out all sorts of emotions in the combatants – both the good and the ugly. Greed and thievery were commonplace, as were kindness and mercy. As the Confederate battle lines swept across the open fields near Shepherdstown, they unloosed an initial volley at the One Hundred and Eighteenth Pennsylvania. The sudden shower of Minié balls mortally wounded Capt. Joseph W. Ricketts and felled several other officers and men. A lightly wounded Pvt. William L. Gabe laid down his musket and tried to assist the stricken Ricketts, who pleaded that Gabe leave him and save himself. At first believing that he was a victim of errant fire from his own men, Captain Ricketts lived long enough to see the gray tide sweep through his position. Gabe, loyal to his commander, refused to leave and was captured by stragglers after the assault wave had passed by. He was appalled to witness some of his captors, against his strong protests, rifling through the body of Ricketts and appropriating his watch, money, and his sword. They stole his coat, vest, and his boots. About the only personal item not taken was Ricketts' personal diary, which one of the thieves handed to the stunned and angry Gabe.

History of the 118th Pennsylvania Volunteers: Corn Exchange Regiment... (Philadelphia: J. L. Smith, 1905).

**

Intermingled with the terror and pathos of battle were moments that the men long remembered as humorous or ironic. One member of Company K of the One Hundred and Eighteenth Pennsylvania, Pvt. John Burke, had received a buckshot pellet in his leg during the fight at Shepherdstown. Despite his pain, he had managed to make it back across the river to safety on the Maryland side, where he sought medical attention. The regimental surgeon extracted the shot and handed Burke a quinine pill before suturing the open wound. So green and naïve was Burke that he innocently inquired, "What shall I do with it, doctor? Should I put it into the hole?" His comrades roared with laughter, breaking the tension of a long day.

History of the 118th Pennsylvania Volunteers: Corn Exchange Regiment... (Philadelphia: J. L. Smith, 1905).

**

The Union troops tumbled back across the Potomac to safety in Maryland, where they were exposed to periodic fire from Rebel sharpshooters on September 21 and 22. Gen. Gouverneur K. Warren, later to be a hero at Gettysburg, coolly ignored this sniping and ordered his brigade to drill in a drained section of the Chesapeake & Ohio Canal paralleling the Potomac, while the enemy's pickets amused themselves by firing at the men and officers. Warren, undaunted, continued the maneuvers.

Alfred Davenport, *Camp and Field Life of the Fifth New York Volunteer Infantry: (Duryee Zouaves).* (New York: Dick and Fitzgerald, 1879).

**

Communications in war can be critical, and a regiment's musicians were vital in transmitting orders over the roar of battle. Drummers would often beat out a cadence during combat to help steady and calm the troops, as well as sending specific commands from officers. Often these were youths, many of which were not even teenagers yet. Yet, they were expected to be "Johnny-on-the-spot" when needed, unless specifically released to the rear by their commander.

General Warren was dismayed that many of his brigade's drummers were timid under fire. To steel their nerves, he ordered a trusted veteran officer, Lt. George Guthrie, to take a squad of them across the Potomac to the Confederate side on September 22. Their assigned mission was to retrieve a 12 lb. Napoleon cannon known to have been abandoned by Lee's army during their retreat. The lieutenant armed himself with a large wooden ramrod to "give the boys a gentle reminder once in a while if it was necessary." There is no record of how many whacks Guthrie had to dish out, but the boys later came back to Warren's line "in good order, dragging the cannon after them..." They had indeed spotted some Rebels, but were not harassed in their expedition. However, not long afterwards, a squadron of veteran soldiers sent over to secure a Rebel caisson ended up in a sharp firefight.

Alfred Davenport, *Camp and Field Life of the Fifth New York Volunteer Infantry: (Duryee Zouaves)*. (New York: Dick and Fitzgerald, 1879).

**

Most of the Union army remained around Sharpsburg for days after the battle, draining the area's resources and often straining the relationship with the locals, who only a few days before could never have imagined the human suffering and misery that they would soon see. Some citizens, such as the widow Margaret Shackleford and her two children, returned to find their residences, barns, and buildings damaged, destroyed, or temporarily appropriated for use as field hospitals. Residents throughout the Sharpsburg region responded to the crisis in various ways. Some were openly hostile to the throng of soldiers, or tried to make a buck from their suffering. Many others generously opened their hearts, homes, and larders to help nurse and feed the wounded.

One worthy and venerable old citizen by the name of William P. Reed, rich in worldly possessions, had a heart overflowing with the milk of human kindness. He lived in a tenant house on the Nicodemus farm just north of Sharpsburg. Concerned for the welfare of the wounded, he paid daily visits to the nearby field hospitals, dispensing little delicacies among the suffering. He even opened his own barn for use as an aid station. At night, he offered up "soul stirring appeals in presence of the wounded to the throne of mercy in their behalf." He soon became a camp favorite, and his visits were eagerly anticipated.

On Sunday, Pvt. Alfred Thomas of the Fifth Wisconsin accompanied Capt. John B. Callis of the Seventh Wisconsin to the old man's barn to visit a number of wounded men from the Iron Brigade. As they were passing a wing of the building, their attention was attracted by the impassioned voice of someone fervently praying. Stepping inside the wing, they discovered the old man kneeling by the side of a poor dying soldier whose leg had been amputated. Reed was busily engaged in interceding in prayer on behalf of the stricken soldier. Nearby, another dying man suddenly brought the benevolent old soul's prayers to a dead stop when he exclaimed, "I say old fellow, I wish you would stop that here noise as I have a devil of a headache and I want to go to sleep." Reed, undaunted by the unbeliever's comments, rose from his knees, walked to the door, raised his hands to heaven, and exclaimed "the Lord Jesus have mercy upon that poor sinner's soul." He carried on with his charity and compassion.

Reed's generosity was not limited to the injured and dying soldiers. Battery B of the Fourth U.S. Artillery had lost several horses at Antietam. Reed, upon hearing of this, presented the company with six of his finest horses, free of charge.

Grant County (Wisconsin) *Herald*, September 24, 1862.

**

Surgeons, assistants, stewards, visiting civilian doctors and nurses – all worked together to comfort the wounded and dying. Lewis Castleman, regimental surgeon of the Fifth Wisconsin, approached one poor wounded Georgian, still lying on the field, who was apparently trying to hide some personal effect from view. Castleman picked it up and gingerly unfolded it. To his surprise, he found it to be a photograph of the Rebel's wife and children. Dr. Castleman, moved with compassion, gently raised the stricken Confederate so that he could better see the image. Their tears soon mingled, as both men realized that the dying soldier would in all likelihood never see his family again. An emotional Castleman wrote in his diary that night, "How easy the graduation from sympathy to affection. I am getting to love these suffering rebels."

Alfred L. Castleman, *The Army of the Potomac: Behinds the Scenes: A Diary of Unwritten History...* (Milwaukee: Strickland & Co., 1863).

**

Lt. John "Jack" Adams of the Nineteenth Massachusetts had been frantic with worry. He had not seen his brother since the confused fighting at Antietam, where his sibling had been stationed at the extreme left of the regiment during its advance. When the regiment finally halted, regrouped, and called muster by company, his brother had not answered. With his anxiety growing, Adams spent all day on September 18 searching the field hospitals in the Union rear to no avail. With the Confederates finally gone from Sharpsburg on September 19, Adams decided to walk around the section of the battlefield that had been under their control. His perseverance paid off, as he located his brother and two comrades near an old haystack. Adams examined his brother and discovered that he had been shot through the right side of his neck, the bullet passing into his left shoulder and severing his spinal column, leaving him unable to move his hands or feet.

A grieving Adams flagged down an ambulance and had his brother carried back to a field hospital, later calling it the "saddest duty of my life." He and his brother had often encouraged one another with the mutual hope that they would be reunited with their family after the war around the old fireside. Alas, it was not to be. Adams would need to write his mother that one of the three boys who had joined the army would not be returning.

Now, his brother was failing, and Adams knelt by his side to hear his last words. A woman's gentle voice softly called out, "Is he your brother?" Adams affirmed the inquiry and ruefully remarked that, as an officer, he must return to his company and look after his men, but he could not bear the thought of leaving his brother to die alone. The lady, who turned out to be Mrs. Mary Lee of Philadelphia, was the mother of a soldier in the same army. With tears streaming down her face, she consoled Adams and promised she would stay with his brother until he died, and would then make sure he had a proper burial. She fulfilled her commitment, and, years after the war, Adams visited her in Philadelphia to extend his gratitude.

In 1896, Adams was awarded the Medal of Honor for his actions at Fredericksburg in December 1862.

John G. B. Adams, *Reminiscences of the Nineteenth Massachusetts Regiment.* (Boston: Wright, Potter Printing Company, 1899).

**

The damage was not confined to the battlefield. According to Pvt. Alfred Thomas of the Iron Brigade's Fifth Wisconsin, "Butternut chivalry, which boasts of its noble bearing and honorable mode of warfare, established a reputation in Sharpsburg for being the most accomplished rascals and burglars that ever disgraced the State with their presence. They broke into private dwellings, robbed the occupants of everything in the way of clothing and eatables; one wantonly destroyed their household furniture."

Grant County (Wisconsin) *Herald*, September 24, 1862.

**

Among the hardest hit were the families whose prosperous farms lay closest to the combat. William Roulette, whose bees had chased off part of the One Hundred and Thirty-second Pennsylvania, later filed a damage claim for his personal losses. His rail fences were almost all gone, used for firewood. Dozens of personal possessions were missing from his house. The harvest had been good, and Roulette, like his neighbors, was in the process of storing vast quantities of food for the upcoming winter. His lengthy list of stolen items included 220 bushels of apples,155 bushels of potatoes, 3 barrels of flour, 8 hogs, 12 sheep, and 3 calves, all destined to be consumed by hungry soldiers instead of by his family.

Files of the National Park Service.

**

Visitors, from the lowly to the mighty, flocked to the battlefield, most hoping to give assistance in some small manner. Andrew G. Curtin, the Governor of Pennsylvania, was among these out-of-towners who arrived in Sharpsburg shortly after the battle. Curtin discovered a member of the Twenty-eighth Ohio lying badly wounded in the arm. He lifted the injured soldier into an awaiting ambulance, the blood dripping from the Buckeye staining the Governor's hands and clothing. The grateful soldier had slipped a little ring to the governor and softly told him to wear it. Curtin soon went on his way, the ring on his finger as promised.

Much later, Curtin was visiting Philadelphia when a young woman called on him. When she was introduced, the lady startled Curtin by placing a kiss on his forehead and expressed great joy at meeting the governor. "Madame," he inquired, "to whom am I indebted for this unexpected salutation?" She sat in a chair, recounted the story of Curtin's visit to Antietam, and jogged his memory of the incident with the fallen Ohio volunteer. Still puzzled, Curtin asked if the soldier had been her husband, brother, father, or son, or even a lover, to which she calmly replied "No, sir" to each inquiry. "Who then, could it be?" finally came the response from an exasperated Curtin.

Referring to the ring which Curtin still wore on his little finger, she mentioned that the band should have the initials C.E.D on it. An inquisitive Curtin pulled off the ring and, indeed, those exact letters were inscribed on the inside. By now thoroughly confused, he gently asked the lady if the ring had been given to her by a soldier that she loved. The woman replied that indeed it had, and the man had been killed at Antietam. She remarked, "He had more love for his country than for me; I honor him for it. That soldier who placed that little ring on your finger stands before you."

With that startling exclamation, she rose from her chair, stood before the astonished governor, and introduced herself as Catherine E. Davidson of Sheffield, Ohio. She had indeed been engaged, but her fiancée had joined the army in response to President Lincoln's call to arms. She had disguised herself and enlisted, but in a different regiment than her betrothed. He had died at Antietam and, ironically, she had been wounded in the same battle. It was her that Curtin had assisted into the ambulance that September day. The lady and the governor spent a pleasant hour reminiscencing before she departed.

Frank Moore, *Anecdotes, Poetry, and Incidents of the War: North and South. 1860-1865.* (New York: Publication office, Bible house, J. Porteus, agent, 1867).

**

As Lee's army retired deeper into Virginia, they were often assailed on their rear and flanks by Federal troops, which frequently sparred with Stuart's cavalry. After crossing the Potomac River, the horse artillery under Capt. John Pelham occasionally would unlimber and throw a few rounds into their pursuers. Pelham kept one gun to the rear, well in advance of his remaining pieces. On one occasion, as Yankees closed in on this particular gun, Stuart ordered the youthful Pelham to retire, but the boy dawdled to fire off a final round. The artillery crewmen began to run to the rear, abandoning the gun. However, Pelham refused to lose the gun. By now all alone, he mounted one of the lead horses to haul the gun to safety. A volley from the Federals dropped the horse, and Pelham coolly cut the traces and mounted another in the six-horse team. He galloped off, but soon, his new horse was also cut down, as was a third soon after he mounted it. Undaunted, and still stubbornly trying to save the cannon, he again cut the traces, and ignoring the whizzing bullets, finally dashed back to Stuart's main line with the three remaining horses and the gun. It was no wonder Stuart admired "the gallant Pelham" so much. Promoted to major, Pelham was killed in action the following spring at Kelly's Ford.

Ben La Bree, *Camp Fires of the Confederacy: A Volume of Humorous Anecdotes, Reminiscences, Deeds of Heroism,...* (Louisville, Kentucky: The Courier-Journal Job Printing Company, 1898).

**

Another Confederate soldier faced a different kind of danger. Chambersburg, Pennsylvania, had been "thrown into the wildest state of excitement" on September 22 by the arrival of the First Maryland Cavalry. They were escorting fifty or sixty "Secesh" prisoners, along with a long train of ninety-one Rebel ammunition wagons that had been captured that morning between Hagerstown and Williamsport, Maryland. A large

92

contingent of Federal cavalry had refused to surrender at Harper's Ferry and had cut their way through Rebel lines to safety. Along the way, they had seized the Confederate wagon train, all without losing a man. The First Maryland Cavalry had been detailed to deliver the prize to Federal authorities.

Among the chagrined Rebel prisoners was Pvt. Clegget Fitzhugh, a native of Hughes Furnace, a small hamlet in Fulton County not far from Chambersburg. Only a few days before, he left his home and traveled to Hagerstown, Maryland to meet the approaching Rebel army. Fitzhugh had enlisted, one of the few Pennsylvanians to respond to Lee's call to arms he had delivered in Frederick on September 8. Somehow, Fitzhugh had gotten wind of the announcement and had cast his lot with the Confederacy. A Rebel less than two weeks, he was now a prisoner of war and back in his home county.

The feeling against Fitzhugh was intense, and an angry crowd cried out "Hang him," "Shoot him," "Kill him," but he was hurried off to prison by the escorting Union officers. The mob finally dispersed, satisfied that the better way was to let the law have its course. Fitzhugh and the other prisoners wound up in an eastern fort under lock and key. He was but one of over one hundred Pennsylvanians who had traveled into neighboring Maryland to enlist in the Confederate service, many to avoid being drafted into the Union army.

Chambersburg *Valley Spirit*, September 24, 1862.
John Esten Cooke, *The Life of Stonewall Jackson*. (New York: Charles B. Richardson, 1863).

**

A different kind of danger lurked, as both armies tried to replenish their vastly depleted ranks shortly after Antietam. One Confederate cavalry company, camped near the Potomac River, was frequently engaged throughout the border between northern Virginia and Maryland in seeking out and arresting men of conscript age who were dodging the officers of the law. It was an area where both secessionists and loyal Union men abounded in fairly equal numbers, and both armies at times claimed the same men. One day the squadron suddenly encountered a particular draft dodger they were seeking along a remote road near his house. When the army sergeant asked the man why he was not in the army, the emboldened man replied, "I never did anything to bring about this war, and I ain't a going to help carry it on." The soldiers ordered the man to accompany them, and his arrogance wilted at the sight of the pistols. "Gentlemen, don't put me in the army. I am the father of three children," he pleaded. This had no affect on the sergeant, who had strict orders to bring in the man. However, he allowed the farmer to say goodbye to his family. The soldiers escorted the man into his home.

When the man's wife learned what was about to occur, she wailed pitifully, a howling soon joined by the children, and the conscript soon cried as well. "Oh," said his wife, "I'd rather see him in his grave!" "Don't bother yourself," replied a heartless soldier, "You won't be disappointed long." With that sarcastic retort, the crying intensified and the room was filled with the pitiful wails. "Oh, stop this nonsense!" shouted the sergeant. "The bullet ain't made that'll kill him; a four-horse team couldn't drag him into a fight." Turning to his prisoner, he intoned, "Aren't you ashamed of yourself to be blubbering like a baby?" The frightened conscript replied, "I wish I was a baby, and a gal baby, too." Sobbing, he was soon led away by the cavalrymen. Two weeks later, he escaped, but was soon recaptured. Undaunted, he again escaped and disappeared into obscurity.

Ben La Bree, *Camp Fires of the Confederacy: A Volume of Humorous Anecdotes, Reminiscences, Deeds of Heroism,...* (Louisville, Kentucky: The Courier-Journal Job Printing Company, 1898).

**

Shortly after the battle of Antietam, General Lee called together his staff, teasingly smiled, and invited, "Come and join me in my tent! I've had something pretty good sent to me. It's in a jug, and the man who presented it to me told me that it was the very best that the country about here produces." The officers and aides eagerly accepted his invitation, some expecting some fine local whiskey. "Thanks to you, General! Show us the quality of it," they responded. Some of Lee's inner circle knew that the general abhorred strong drink, and were quite suspicious of his mysterious smile. A circle of soldiers soon surrounded "Marse Robert," each holding out a battered, rusty tin cup. Lee, with much gravity and care, as if each drop was precious, slowly raised the jug and uncorked it. The crowd pressed in as he very deliberately poured out some of its contents into the first man's waiting cup – fresh buttermilk! "There!" he smugly declared, "That's the best this country can produce! I hope that you will enjoy it." The lack of whiskey notwithstanding, the Rebels reveled in this rare piece of levity from their commander, who was usually too heavily burdened with care to relax in this manner.

Bradley Gilman, *Robert E. Lee.* (New York: The Macmillan Company, 1915).

**

For most of the soldiers, it was now time to contemplate the sights and scenes of Antietam, and reflect on what had occurred, and the significance (or insignificance) of life. Rev. A. D. Betts, the chaplain of the Thirtieth North Carolina, had constantly ministered to the wounded and dying during Lee's retreat into Virginia. On September 22, he had ridden to the rear in the wagon train to rest. He soon took time to introspectively examine his own experience. "Five years ago this afternoon my second son, Willie, was born. God bless him and spare us to see each other. Ride to Martinsburg in afternoon. Lie beside my horse at night, gazing at the stars and thinking of Mary and my little ones. 'What is man, that Thou art mindful of him?'" Betts survived the war to return home to his family. Tens of thousands, blue and gray alike, were not as fortunate.

Rev. Alexander D. Betts, *Experience of a Confederate Chaplain, 1861-1864.* (Greenville, SC, 1900s). University of North Carolina library, Call number C970.78 B56e 190?.

Simmering sectional rivalries soon resurfaced. As a patrol from the Eleventh Pennsylvania foraged at one Bakersville, Maryland farm for a dinner of Shanghai roosters, they had an animated conversation with the farm's elderly matron. She was perfectly willing to share her food and larder with the Union soldiers, but she did not take too kindly to the Rebel invasion of her region, thinking many of them to be arrogant and condescending. She complained, "Them Virginians always thought they were a heap smarter than the Marylanders. But I told them they had better stay at home; that they would find out to their sorrow that we had just as smart people here as they had over there. I always said this fight would come someday. But they (the Virginians) always said I was dumb, and didn't know anything."

In contrast to this feeling, the aura of Southern invincibility had finally been broken. One Rebel surgeon, a Virginian, had been left behind at Boonsboro after the fighting at South Mountain to care for the hundred or so wounded from his regiment. He resignedly remarked to the Eleventh Pennsylvania's chaplain, William Locke, "Our recent successes over your army have made us too confident. We had no thought of being driven from South Mountain…"

William Henry Locke, *The Story of the Regiment*. (Philadelphia: J. B. Lippincott & Co., 1868).

The United States Christian Commission and other volunteers from around the North stayed for weeks near Sharpsburg ministering to the wounded, spreading the gospel, and assisting in whatever way they could. One day, Edward Smith and other USCC men were burying several bodies. They were assisted by a talkative Union soldier who was telling them how he had emerged from the battle unscathed. He concluded, "For which I thank God!" A nearby man cynically commented, "Thank the rebels for being such bad marksmen!"

Rev. Edward P. Smith, *Incidents of the United States Christian Commission*. (Philadelphia: J. B. Lippincott & Co., 1869).

One Federal artillerist, later to gain prominence as a brigadier general and military strategist, gushed over his experiences in a letter to his sister ten days after the battle. Col. Emory Upton, with a definite lust for the soldier's life, wrote, "The pleasant campaign of Maryland has closed with the expulsion of the rebel invaders…, I never spent any hours more agreeably or enjoyed myself better. We lived well, marched through a lovely country, had beautiful weather, magnificent scenery, and above all two glorious battles."

Peter S. Michie, *The Life and Letters of Emory Upton*. (New York: D. Appleton and Company, 1885).

**

Totally opposite to Upton's exuberance for campaigning was the cowardly attitude of an unnamed Union soldier encountered sixty days after Antietam by Brig. Gen. George Gordon. While inspecting the region, he spotted the uniformed man lounging in the doorway of a rather common farmhouse near the battlefield. As the army had long since moved into Virginia, there should not have been a lone soldier in that spot in November, unless he was a deserter. An inquisitive Gordon rode up and asked him, "What are you doing here?" The soldiers claimed he had been detailed by his colonel to guard the house from looting, and, since the colonel had never returned to formally relieve him, the soldier had to stay there, enjoying the safety and comfort of the rear lines (and hospitality of the host family). By now irate, Gordon ordered "this sneaking coward to strap on his knapsack and start for his regiment." Gordon soon rounded up dozens of other skulkers and similarly sent them back to the front lines.

George H. Gordon, *A War Diary of Events in the War of the Great Rebellion 1863-1865*. (Boston: James R. Osgood and Company, 1882).

**

The surgeon of the Thirteenth South Carolina, Dr. Spencer Welch, missed the fighting at Antietam, as he had become violently sick during the march from Virginia and had recuperated at a private house. Joining the regiment the day after the battle, he had since moved with the regimental wounded to a hospital at Charles Town, Virginia. He considered himself fortunate, as, between he and his brother, "He and I have three flannel shirts between us, and I have some other very good clothing. I have but one pair of socks, and they are nearly worn out. I had a good pair, but some one stole them."

Life in the rear lines was still dangerous. He added, "The Yankees came near enough the other day to throw several shells into town, but they did no harm except to wound a little boy. They are certainly fanatical. As much as we whip them, they are not disposed to give up. The people here – especially the women – hate them very much."

Spencer Glasgow Welch, *A Confederate Surgeon's Letters to His Wife*. (New York and Washington: The Neale Publishing Company, 1911).

**

With the battle over and the Confederates back in Virginia, hundreds of visitors flocked to Sharpsburg from all across the North. Many came with sorrowful hearts in search of loved ones who were reported either wounded or dead. On the other hand, hundreds more were curiosity seekers who viewed the blood-stained fields merely to behold the ghastly and mutilated forms of the dead and "to note every tree, fence, rock and house struck by the dread messenger of death which had been belched forth from the cannon. Among this class of visitors, a perfect mania for relics possessed them. Pieces of shells, broken bayonets, canteens, knapsacks, cannon balls, splinters from fences and trees struck by shot are seized upon and carried off in triumph. Had it been possible, I believe some of these relic hunters would have carried off a dead 'Secesh.'"

Letter from Alfred Thomas to the Grant County (Wisconsin) *Herald*, September 24, 1862.

**

Sometimes people do things that are just plain stupid. In late September, the Union army had reoccupied Harper's Ferry with fresh troops, among them Battery A, First Rhode Island Light Artillery. The Nineteenth Maine Infantry was camped nearby on Bolivar Heights. This regiment "had the largest men in it that I ever saw," according to artilleryman Tom Aldrich. However, apparently their brains did not match their brawn. The Maine boys marched to the top of the heights and stacked arms near mealtime. During the fall of Harper's Ferry two weeks before, a battery of 20 lb. Parrott Rifles had occupied that position, and several discarded shells were still lying about. Without checking to see if the rounds were still live, several Maine lumberjacks soon used the shells to construct a fireplace to set their frying pans on. Soon they had a nice fire started and began preparing their food. The heat soon set off some of the shells, with fierce explosions ringing the air.

Assuming they were under a sudden Confederate surprise attack, the large regiment panicked and stampeded back down the hill, looking for cover. The nearby Rhode Island battery sprang into place, ready to return fire. Soon, the source of the "bombardment" was discovered, and everyone could laugh at the lumberjacks from Maine. Luckily, no one was killed in the mishap, and only a few men were slightly injured by the flying shell fragments.

Thomas M. Aldrich, *The History of Battery A, First Regiment Rhode Island Light Artillery.* (Providence: Snow & Farnham, 1904).

**

On the Federal side, frustrations mounted in Washington with Maj. Gen. George McClellan's inability to decisively defeat the Confederate army. President Lincoln had for some time been concerned that McClellan loved his army too much to sacrifice it if need be to once and for all whip Lee's veterans. His attitude was perhaps best expressed by a story told by Ozias M. Hatch of Springfield, Illinois, who had accompanied his friend Lincoln on a visit to McClellan's camp. They spent the night in an army tent, and, rising early in the crisp morning, Lincoln suggested that they take a walk about the camp before sunrise. The pair inspected the immense campsite, the troops' quarters, the artillery, and all the appurtenances of the majestic army. Lincoln was in a pensive mood, and not a word was spoken for quite some time.

Finally, just as the sun was rising and dissipating the morning fog, the duo reached the top of a hill with a commanding view of the vast gathering of Federal military might. The President paused, placed his left hand on Hatch's shoulder, and

97

slowly and deliberately waved his right hand in the direction of the great city of white tents. With a serious tone, he inquired, "Mr. Hatch, what is all this before us?" A puzzled Hatch replied, "Why, Mr. President, this is General McClellan's army." "No, Mr. Hatch, no," Lincoln sarcastically responded, "this is General McClellan's body-guard."

Shelby M. Cullom (U.S. Senator from Illinois), *Fifty Years of Public Service.* (Chicago: A. C. McClurg & Co., 1911).

**

Soldiers from Company A of the One Hundred and Twenty-sixth Pennsylvania, still encamped near Sharpsburg in early October, had the monotony of camp life broken by an unusual incident. Cpl. Emmanuel Forney was crossing a particular nearby field when he discovered sticking up from the freshly turned earth an iron object that he presumed to be a portion of a shell or round shot. Curious, he kicked it with his foot and began clearing away some of the surrounding dirt. To his surprise, he soon recognized the mysterious protruding object as the knob on the breech of a large cannon. An excited Forney, who was known for his wit and tendency to exaggerate, raced to his company and delivered the news of his find. He finally fetched his disbelieving comrades, who soon exhumed the great prize – a magnificent Parrott gun tube, apparently buried by the retreating Rebels. The exultant Pennsylvanians triumphantly carried their captured cannon to regimental headquarters, and Forney was celebrated throughout the camp. The boys of Company A declared that this was the first enemy cannon they had captured, and they were determined it would not be the last.

Now, everyone else in the regiment wanted his own share of the glory, and a rumor quickly spread that the field contained several other buried artillery pieces. "A perfect furor after buried cannon" seized the regiment, and soon holes in several neighboring fields were being dug down to a distance of several feet. Several soldiers, owing to a scarcity of spades and shovels, soon wore their nails to the quick by digging with their bare hands in the forlorn hope of being the next lucky one to locate a hidden gun tube.

According to one eyewitness, "It is astonishing how reports become exaggerated. The first rumor your correspondent heard of the cannon finding, was to the effect that 'Mawny Forney had found six twelve pound Parrott guns, and had just carried them all into camp.' The corporal, it will be remembered, is five feet two, and weighs something near a hundred. The report *did* sound rather improbable, but as Forney is capable of almost anything, we followed the crowd and soon learned the true state of the case."

Chambersburg *Valley Spirit*, October 8, 1862.

**

As both sides resumed the monotony and routine, occasionally the picket lines were so close that the enemy soldiers were within earshot of one another. They often verbally sparred and jostled each other. Noting that the distant Confederate pickets were dressed in Union-issued jackets, one Ninth New Hampshire boy inquired as to where the Rebs had acquired their blue overcoats. The Rebel taunted, "We took them off the dead Yankees at Antietam. Why didn't you take ours?" The New Englander shot back, "Because they walked off so fast!" The sometimes profane, sometimes jovial repartee continued throughout the day, the great battle being refought with words and insults instead of bullets.

David Wright Judd, *The Story of the Thirty-third N. Y. S. Vols., Or, Two Years Campaigning in Virginia and Maryland.* (Rochester: Benton & Andrews, 1864).

**

When in late October, Lincoln received a dispatch from General McClellan complaining that he could not pursue Lee due to "sore-tongued and fatigued horses," the president sarcastically responded, "Will you pardon me for asking what the horses of your army have done since Antietam that fatigues anything?" Within a few weeks, McClellan was fired by Lincoln and replaced by Ambrose Burnside. The seemingly constant merry-go-round of Federal generals continued.

Charles E. Davis, *Three Years in the Army: The Story of the Thirteenth Massachusetts Volunteers.* (Estes and Lauriat, 1894)

**

The lingering effects of the battle were evident for months and even years after the armies left. For one Sharpsburg family, the battle caused a particularly poignant set of tragedies. Adam and Nancy Michael owned the 81-acre Green Hill Farm, which had been riddled by long-range Union artillery shells. The couple had lost their crops, livestock, and all of the apples from their orchard. All the fencing had been burned for fuel by the Yankees, and the house and barn used as a crude field hospital for up to ninety wounded soldiers. Bodies were periodically carried from the parlor (which now looked like a "hog pen") and buried in a nearby field. The property loss was estimated at $2,000, but the real cost was yet to come.

The Michaels had previously lost a sixteen-year-old daughter before the war. Now, three family members became seriously ill with typhoid fever caused by the unsanitary conditions. On October 24, one of the Michael girls, Elizabeth, died from complications of typhoid. One month after her daughter died, Nancy Michael also succumbed to the disease. The last daughter, Kate, never completely recovered from typhoid and finally died in August 1864, not quite two years after the battle.

Letter of Samuel Michael to his brother David in Indianapolis, *Washington Times*, January 3, 2004.

**

Lee's Maryland Campaign was over, although his desire to invade the North was unabated. He would try again nine months later in what became the Gettysburg

Campaign. However, for now, his men remained confident in their leader and what the future held. Artilleryman Robert Stiles of the Charlottesville Artillery stated:

It was by no means admitted among intelligent Confederate soldiers that the only or the main design of the first Maryland campaign was to stir up revolt in Maryland or to recruit our army by enlistments there. It is not disputed that these may have been among the objects sought to be accomplished, nor that, so far as this is true, the campaign was a failure. The Confederate view of the matter, from a military standpoint, is in brief this:

"By our invasion of Maryland we cleared Virginia of enemies, sending them home to defend their own capital and their own borders. We subsisted our army for a time outside our own worn-out territory. We gathered large quantities of badly-needed supplies, to a great extent fitting out our troops with improved firearms, in place of the old smoothbore muskets, and replacing much of our inferior field artillery with improved guns."

To many undeterred Confederates, the Maryland Campaign had been a success. To a relieved George McClellan, it had been an abject failure for Lee's army. To Abraham Lincoln, it had been the opening that he needed to issue his Emancipation Proclamation.

Robert Stiles, *Four Years Under Marse Robert*. (New York: The Neale Publishing Company, 1904).

**

Years after the war, veterans would meet at reunions and in public, to regale one another with tales of their heroism in the "late unpleasantness." Deeds were magnified and exaggerated as the former soldiers tried to impress each other with their valor and courage. Others sought to extend thanks for kindnesses extended during the war.

A former lieutenant in the Sixteenth Virginia, [presumed by this author to be George H. Jordan], was walking down a street in Richmond one day when he was accosted by a half soldier, half beggar, with a most reverential military salute. With a thick Irish brogue, the unkempt man intoned, "God bless your honor and long life to you!" When the former officer asked the Irishman how he knew him, he replied that he most certainly recognized the man who had saved his life in battle. The ex-lieutenant, self-satisfied and feeling a little proud to have such recognition of his wartime valor, pressed a fifty-cent piece into the beggar's hand and asked him the occasion when he had saved the man's life. The beggar replied, "Sure, it was at Antietam, when, seeing your honor run away, as fast as your legs would carry you, from the enemy, I followed your lead and ran after you out of the way, whereby, under God, you saved my life! Oh, good luck to your honor! I will never forget it or you!" The much chagrined officer walked away.

Dr. Linus P. Brockett, *The Camp, the Battle Field, and the Hospital: Or, Lights and Shadows of the Great Rebellion.* (National Publishing Company, 1866).

**

     For hundreds of other veterans, Antietam remained a source of constant pain and misery for the rest of their lives. Ernst J. Krieger was a 29-year-old captain in the Seventh Ohio Volunteer Infantry at Antietam. Born in Germany, he had sailed to Cleveland with his parents at a young age. There, he became involved in the "Turner" movement, societies and clubs for German immigrants that combined gymnastics, politics, and military drills. When war broke out, he enlisted in a three-month regiment as a private, and then, in June 1861, joined the newly raised Seventh Ohio Volunteer Infantry (OVI), a regiment with a term of enlistment of three years, rising to captain for gallantry in action. At Antietam, he was wounded in the head not far from Dunker Church, but survived to fight again at Chancellorsville, Gettysburg, and in the Atlanta Campaign. After mustering out in the summer of 1864 when his enlistment term expired, he became the major of the One Hundred and Seventy-seventh OVI until the end of the war. Returning home in mid-1865, Krieger became a partner in a machine building firm in Cleveland, but the business eventually failed. By then, he had suffered numerous attacks of paralysis resulting from his Antietam head wound, and the veteran was finally admitted to the Soldiers Home in Dayton, Ohio, in 1878. Failing rapidly, Krieger died three years later at the age of forty-eight, his story being just one of hundreds of men whose lives were physically or emotionally impaired and finally cut short by Antietam. The Bloodiest Day had claimed yet another victim.

Lawrence Wilson, *Itinerary of the Seventh Ohio Volunteer Infantry 1861-1864.* (New York and Washington: The Neale Publishing Company, 1907).

Wilson's book, mentioned above, also contains the following poem, a fitting memorial to the now still fields along Antietam Creek…

Antietam.
By Irene Fowler Brown

Shock and onset of gray and blue,
   Smoke and carnage and spatter of red,
Belching cannon where young corn grew,
   Rank after rank of weltering dead.
Here in the valley they charged and met,
   South and North – and the slain piled deep;
Here in the valley the grass grew wet,
   Thousands were left on the field asleep.

And why this Antietam? The Bloody Lane
  Where cattle browse on their homeward way,
And loitering plowmen to tinkling chain
  Follow the path of dying day.
Peace and plenty and lights of home,
  Planting and harvesting and even-song,
Flower and fruit from the blood-soaked loam,
  Bounteous corn-fields where Death reaped long.

O my heart! Wilt thou look and learn?
  Out of havoc and blood and strife,
See, where the red of the sod we turn
  Blossoms the grace of a strange new life.
Sorrow and pain and hatred will go,
  Sharpness of death – that, too, will cease,
Out of the agony, roses grow;
  Out of the heart-ache, infinite peace.

About the Author

Scott L. Mingus, Sr. is a scientist and executive in the paper and printing industry, and holds patents in self-adhesive postage stamp products and in bar code labels. Mingus has written for *Gettysburg Magazine, The Zouave, Charge!, The Herald,* and numerous other military history and wargaming publications. He is the author of *Human Interest Stories of the Gettysburg Campaign* and *Flames Beyond Gettysburg: The Gordon Expedition,* the first full-length treatment of John B. Gordon's Georgia brigade during the Gettysburg Campaign.

Mingus has written several books on wargaming the Civil War, including the two-volume *Enduring Valor: Gettysburg in Miniature,* the popularly acclaimed *Undying Courage: The Antietam Campaign in Miniature, Touched With Fire,* and *Crossed Sabers: Gettysburg in Miniature.* His latest work, *My Brother's Keeper,* will be published in late 2007 with over a dozen new wargaming scenarios for the Gettysburg campaign for skirmish-level wargaming. He and his wife Debi are the editors and publishers of *Charge!,* an international magazine for Civil War miniature wargamers.

A native of southern Ohio, Mingus attended Miami University in Oxford, Ohio, completing his undergraduate degree in Paper Science and Engineering in 1978. He is married to his high school sweetheart, Deborah (Ferrell) Mingus, and they have three adult children (Scott, Tom, and Melissa), daughter-in-law Becky, and a grandson, Tristan. Mingus spent 23 years working for office products giant Avery Dennison near Cleveland, Ohio, before joining the P.H. Glatfelter Company, a global manufacturer of specialty papers, in 2001. He and his wife now reside in York, Pennsylvania, and attend the Stillmeadow Church of the Nazarene.

****

Other Books by Colecraft:

Civil War Artillery at Gettysburg
Philip M. Cole

Command and Communication Frictions in the Gettysburg Campaign
Philip M. Cole

Human Interest Stories of the Gettysburg Campaign
Scott L. Mingus, Sr.

Colecraft website: www.colecraftbooks.com

e-mail: colecraftbooks@aol.com

Printed in the United States
72668LV00001B/5-154

9 780977 712533